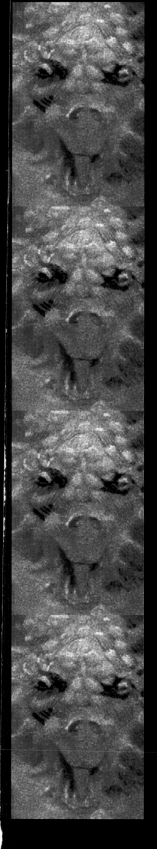

Illustrated Novels:
A New Art Form for a New Age

They say a picture's worth a thousand words... and they're right. As anyone who's seen a movie and then read the book it's based on can tell you, every media has its own strengths, things it can do better than any other form. And that's what Illustrated Novels bring: the strengths of two different media—strong, elegant, cinematic prose and detailed illustrations that speak volumes to the reader.

The power of prose combined with the beauty of rich illustrations.

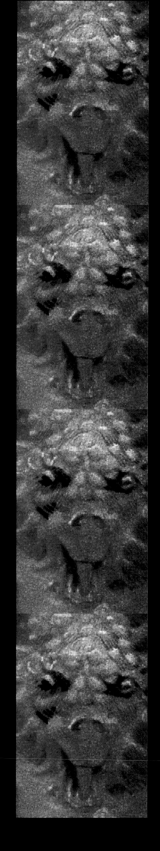

MARGARET WEIS'
TESTAMENT OF THE
DRAGON

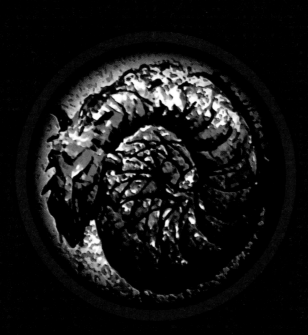

CREATED BY MARGARET WEIS
AND DAVID BALDWIN

AN ILLUSTRATED NOVEL

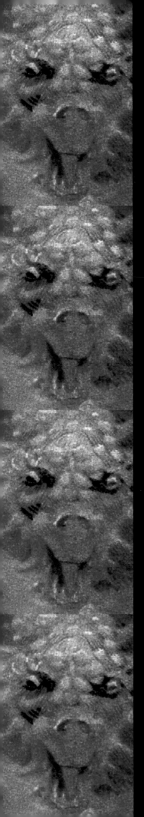

HarperPrism

A Division of HarperCollins*Publishers*
10 East 53rd Street, New York, N.Y., 10022

Designed by Michael Chatham

HarperPrism books may be purchased for educational, business, or sales promotional use. For information, please write: Special Markets Department, HarperCollins Publishers, 10 East 53rd Street, New York, NY 10022-5299.

ISBN: 0-06-105543-3

Printed in the United States of America
First Printing: August 1997

97 98 99 00 01 ❖/RRD 10 9 8 7 6 5 4 3 2 1

MARGARET WEIS'
TESTAMENT OF THE
DRAGON

INTRODUCTION

I WAS BORN TO DARKNESS IN THE TIME OF THE PLAGUE, WHEN DEATH AND DESPAIR FILLED ALL OF EUROPE AND THE STENCH OF ROTTING FLESH TAINTED THE AIR OF AN ENTIRE CONTINENT. NOT EVEN ENGLAND, PROTECTED BY WATER ON ALL SIDES, OR THE WALLS IN THE HOUSE OF A DISTINGUISHED ENGLISH LORD COULD DEFY THE BLACK DEATH. MY ENTIRE FAMILY FELL BEFORE IT, UNTIL ONLY MY WIFE AND I REMAINED TO LAY BLISTERED AND DYING IN OUR FORSAKEN MANOR.

IT WAS THEN THAT I CHOSE DARKNESS.

DARKNESS AND IMMORTALITY. FOR THE CREATURE TO WHOM I PLEDGED MY SOUL, THE DRAGON OF THE

WEST, HEALED MY BODY AND GRANTED ME EVERLASTING LIFE SO LONG AS I SERVED HIM. I BECAME THE WYRM, HIS MINION AND ASSASSIN. I BECAME HIS LIVING WEAPON IN HIS BATTLE AGAINST THE DRAGONS BEYOND AND THEIR FAITHFUL FOLLOWERS THE DROKPAS. I BECAME DEATH AND CHAOS.

THAT WAS MANY CENTURIES AGO, AND THE TIME WEIGHS HEAVILY UPON ME, NOW. I LOOK BACK AT THE DECADES OF MY EXISTENCE WITH A WEARY AND, POSSIBLY, WISER EYE. I HAVE BEGUN HERE TO COLLECT RECORDS OF MY DEEDS, TO SET DOWN A CHRONICLE OF THE DRAGON'S WORKS THROUGHOUT HISTORY. AND TO IDENTIFY MY PART IN IT.

THESE TALES ARE BUT A FEW OF THE DIRE ADVENTURES WHICH I HAVE UNDERTAKEN, A MERE TASTE OF THE BLACK LIFE I HAVE LED. FROM THE EARLY DAYS WHEN THE RAW POWER OF THE DRAGON INTOXICATED ME ON THE SHORES OF LOCH NESS TO THE TIME OF THE FRENCH REVOLUTION WHEN I LEARNED THE COST OF MY ARROGANCE AND THE VALUE OF KNOWING ONE'S ENEMIES. TO CHICAGO, ONE OF THE GREATEST CITIES OF THE MODERN WORLD, WHERE MY LIFE IN SERVICE TO THE DRAGON CHANGED DRASTICALLY.

READ THESE ACCOUNTS AND UNDERSTAND THE CREATURE I HAVE BECOME, KNOW THE EXISTENCE I HAVE SUFFERED. I AM SIR JUSTINIAN, EARL OF STERLING... AND HERE BEGINS MY TESTAMENT.

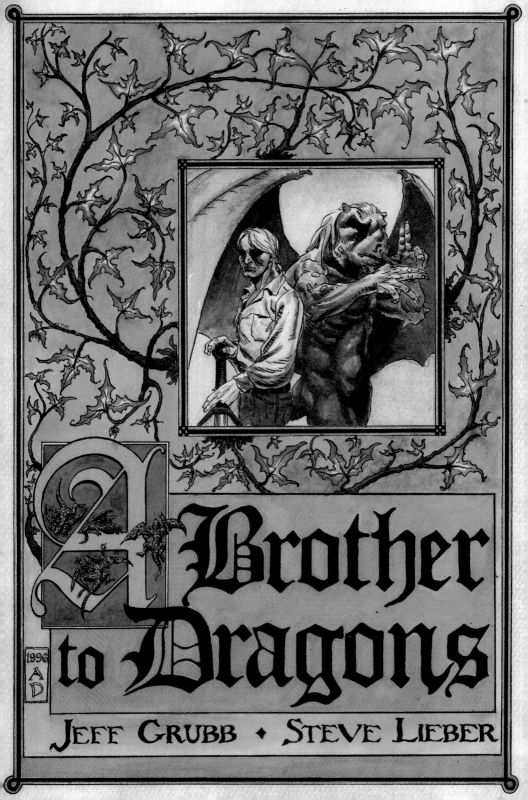

A Brother to Dragons

JEFF GRUBB • STEVE LIEBER

I

𝔵 𝔵 𝔵

THE NIGHT WAS ebony black and overcast, the low clouds lit from below by the milky lights of Chicago's western suburbs. Anyone looking up would probably not see it at all, and if they spotted it, would mistake it for a bat or a night-stranded goose at the altitude at which it flew. None would notice it circling a particular patch of ground, an old barn standing lonely vigil on an untilled farm field.

In the darkness above, the Wyrm circled, watched, and waited.

The barn had been long-abandoned, the property sold to a large realty firm with an ampersanded name. Three years from now, the barn would be gone, replaced with an overly-stylish entrance to an overpriced housing development, one with a name like Deer Creek Commons or Olde Geneva Grove. For now it provided a hiding place, a safe haven for those within.

The ground sloped away from the barn on the far side, the side away from the main road, and there a pair of pick-ups and a compact were hidden from prying eyes. From within the barn there emitted a low drone, which merged with the crickets outside. Few, by accident or design, would bother this gathering.

The barn's interior was illuminated by candles—thick, stubby votaries, stylish dinner table tapers, thin white emergency candles, and scented novelty candles cast in the shapes of wizards, castles, and dragons. The small flames danced and guttered in the slight breeze that managed to weave its way through the weathered lumber of the walls. Two rusted Weber grills, overloaded with charcoal, serving as makeshift braziers, glowed hot and red, framing a solid table of concrete blocks, topped with a large piece of plywood. The inside of the barn walls moved with the tall, flickering shadows of the droning, robed figures.

The group's leader marked symbols with colored chalk on the plywood board with broad, rough strokes. It was a crude approximation of the symbol he had seen in the books. He laid out on the diagram a tarnished silver goblet, a cracked mirror, a small lizard skull, and the shed skin of a snake. He placed at one side of the diagram a pick-like axe, its handle about two feet long, with a narrow, yellowish triangle of a blade rawhide-lashed to its split end.

At the far side of the makeshift altar, opposite the axe, the leader placed a cage made of wire and plastic. Cowering in the back of the cage was a small black kitten, mewling softly, its green eyes wide and frightened.

The leader raised his hands overhead to the other figures. There were eight in addition to the leader, though they cast a legion of shadows against the walls. The droning subsided.

"We gather together to call the powers beyond us," intoned the robed figure, the flames reflecting off his glasses, making them visible beneath the edge of his cowl. "We are here to summon the aspects of the Dragons Beyond."

"Heheh," whispered one of the hooded figures in a low, guttural voice, "He said Ass-pect."

"Shuddup, Stu," said another of the figures.

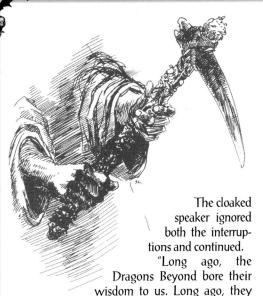

"Power!"

"Make ready the sacrifice!" bellowed the wire-rimmed leader. One of the robed figures, the large one with the Big Johnson shirt, stepped forward and opened the cage. The kitten shrank back to its furthest reaches, and Big Johnson had to struggle to scoop the tiny creature up. The small cat mewled and struggled in his hand. The leader reached for the pick-bladed axe, running a thumb along the yellowed tip and underside. The axe's blade was fashioned like a great serpent's fang, and was razor-sharp.

The wire-rimmed leader turned back to his large companion, who was holding the kitten outwards as if it were a live grenade. "Accept this sacrifice in your name, to allow you to return to us, to share your knowledge and power!"

Big Johnson set the kitten down among the tokens on the diagram, then picked up the goblet to catch the blood, clutching it in both hands. The leader grasped the kitten firmly behind the head with his left hand. He raised the blade over his head to bring it down in a sudden, chopping blow on the small cat.

The kitten squirmed out of the leader's grip, pivoted its head around, and sank its small, needle-sharp teeth into the leader's hand.

"Crap!" he shouted, pulling his hand away and dropping the pick-like axe. The cat did not let loose its grip, instead sinking its teeth deeper into the fleshy ball of the young man's hand, right below the thumb. The black cat increased its attack, digging its claws into the leader's bare arms. Its claws left dark streaks of red. The leader shrieked loudly, "CrapcrapCRAP!"

Propriety and ceremony were immediately forgotten as the group's leader danced behind the makeshift altar, shaking his arm frenetically, trying to knock the kitten loose. Several of the other robed figures laughed, and one or two headed towards the back of the barn, where the beer had been stashed.

The wire-rimmed leader cursed profusely and finally dislodged the cat with a whip-like snap of his arm. The kitten was a dark comet as it flew to a darkened corner. There was a thump and another high-pitched, growling snarl as it landed.

The cloaked speaker ignored both the interruptions and continued.

"Long ago, the Dragons Beyond bore their wisdom to us. Long ago, they gave their gifts to us. Long ago, they sacrificed their might for us. Long ago, they left us to grow and to mature and to learn in wisdom. Now we call upon their wisdom, their gifts, their sacrifice, and appeal for their return."

"Appeal for their return," said the remainder of the cloaked figures, almost in an embarrassed mutter. One or two voices cracked with youth as they said the words.

"They once were among us, and will be among us again," said the robed leader, raising his head upwards to the rafters. The hood fell backwards to reveal a red-haired face, young and clean. Freckles bedecked each cheek beneath his thick wire-rimmed glasses.

"Among us again," chorused the assemblage, stronger this time. A few of them shifted uneasily. They wore Nikes and Gap jeans beneath the robes. One of the hooded robes had fallen open to reveal a "Big Johnson" cartoon on a stained white shirt.

"Come to us, Dragons of Beyond," said the leader, "Come to us in blood and fire!"

"In blood and fire!" repeated the assemblage, now getting into the swing of the ceremony.

"I summon your wisdom!" said the leader.

"Wisdom!"

"I summon your knowledge!"

"Knowledge!"

"I summon your power!"

Wire-rims cursed again and said, "Find the damned cat! We can't go on without it."

The other cultists laughed. "Give it up, Jay," called one.

"Jason, have a brewsky," said another, holding a pale green bottle up in the flickering light.

Jason, the ceremony's leader, pulled himself up to his full, slender height, raising both arms (one streaked with rivulets of blood) above his head in appeal, "I call on the Dragons Beyond! I call on their power! Hear my plea!" His voice cracked as he spoke.

The others laughed at the display, and some of them pulled down their hoods. The faces beneath were all young and male, with a few earring studs and sparse attempts at facial hair their only claim to maturity.

The leader caught the laughter, and slowly lowered his arms, smiling. He sucked on the wound on his hand for a moment, then chuckled. "Better luck next time, I guess."

Something hard and heavy smashed into the wall outside, about five feet above Jason's head. The sound of the impact silenced the

entire group. A few worried faces turned towards the far doorway, still cracked open just a hand's span. Had their little ceremony been found out? Was the farmer who owned the barn out there, or worse yet, the police?

Jason looked up at the sound, dust dislodged from the blow settling on his wire rims. There was a second blow at the same place, just above the loft door. This one rattled the entire barn, and the boards of the loft door began to curve inwards, splintering beneath the force.

Standing next to Jason, Big Johnson started to say something, but it was drowned out by the third blow. This one smashed through the wood of the loft door and the timbers around it. The robed, would-be cultists dodged as large splinters of wood flew among them.

Something huge and dark barreled through the hole, spinning and landing on the altar with splayed, reptilian feet. The assembled props for the ceremony were scattered in all directions.

The new arrival was roughly humanoid, an eight-foot body with huge, gargoyle-like wings. Its skin was similar to an alligator's,

mottled with leathery pustules along the length of its body and limbs. Its twisted flesh glimmered crimson in the light of the Weber grills, its arms and legs ended in taloned claws sharp enough to cleave the light itself. Its face was lizard-like, ending in a short muzzle filled with sharp teeth. It had hair, a white eruption that flowed down its back like a mane. Its eyes glowed of their own hellish radiance and were the color of boiling blood.

Jason looked up and said, "SunovaBITCH! We did it!"

The reptilian creature spun and grabbed the leader by the front of his robes, hefting him up onto the altar.

"No," said the Wyrm, its voice a husky baritone, "You did not."

The creature grasped the leader's head firmly, and with a single swift move, bent it backwards. Jason gave a high-pitched, almost girlish scream which died in a blood-choked gurgle and the deep popping of shattered vertebrae.

The creature let go of Jason's head, leaving it at the impossible angle against his back, and with its free hand ripped the young man's throat open. Blood gushed from the

ragged gash made by the Wyrm's claw, and the creature dropped the young man behind the altar. Jason's lifeless body collapsed like a discarded rag doll.

The others were stunned by the display, but only for a moment. Then they panicked, running towards the large doors at the far side of the barn.

The winged creature leapt down and grabbed the handle of one of the Weber grills. With almost casual ease he hefted the burning brazier overhand at the entrance, catching one of the retreating youths in the back. The young man screamed as the hot coals burned through his robe and into his flesh. The coals scattered among the other fleeing men, setting their robes afire with small, smoky blazes as well.

The draconian beast then sprung, tucking its huge, bat-like wings behind it as it leapt and spun itself in place, such that it landed feet-first, facing his would-be escapees, between them and the door.

The first of the departing cultists tried to stop and turn back, but slipped and went sprawling on the floor. The creature jumped forward, landing with all its weight on the youth. There was the wet-stick sound of a backbone cracking and the soft gurgling of lungs filling with blood. The crushed youth flailed once, then was still.

One of the youths now had a two-by-four, and brought it up in a clumsy stroke, aiming at the creature's head. It struck instead one of the misshapen shoulders, and might have struck a leather sofa for all the effect it seemed to have on the beast. The Wyrm ripped the board out of the youth's hands and drove it through the boy's stomach, hard. The board stayed embedded in the youth's stomach as he fell away from his opponent.

The fire from the spilled coals was now spreading among the scattered straw and dry wood of the barn. Tongues of flame were dancing along the floor, and already climbing up the supports towards the rafters.

Two youths tried to rush past the creature, one on each side. With two sweeping strokes the beast disemboweled the pair of them, and left them to watch their intestines spill out on the dusty floor.

One of the youths, a thin, lanky one with a moustache thin enough to be wishful thinking, fumbled for something in his pocket. He brought it up in both hands, a small gun, a 22 caliber revolver. The creature did not seem to be impressed by the weapon, and slowly strode towards the young man. The mustached youth shouted something that might have been a warning or a prayer, and pulled the trigger.

The soft pop of the gun was drowned out by the creature's snarl. The bullet splashed a small crimson hole in his hide, but did not stop his advance. The mustached youth fired again, and kept on firing until the hammer clicked on empty chambers. By then there was no time or place to run, for the winged beast was on top of him. One clawed hand sank into the youth's belly to hold him in place while the other back-handed him across the jaw. The youth's neck snapped, and he slumped to the floor, his head pointed in an alien direction.

The Wyrm caught him, and carefully broke each of the dying boy's arms. The gunshots stung him, but were already healing over, reduced to mere red tears along his mottled hide.

The others had fled to another, normal-sized door at the far side, slamming into it. The door held, secured earlier from the far side, but that did not prevent them from trying to shoulder it down, driven by their terror and panic.

Almost leisurely, the Wyrm snatched one, cracked the screaming youth over his knee, and tossed the body aside, reaching for another with the practiced mannerism of a chain smoker cycling through cigarettes.

Finally, the panic died with most of the young men. Their blood did little to extinguish the flames, and their clothing only fed the fires.

One was left, cowering by the altar. The youth in the Big Johnson T-shirt. His eyes were wide and teary from the smoke. The creature slouched towards him, and the youth retreated until the flames prevented him from fleeing further. The creature reached out with both hands, softly and firmly gripping the boy by both sides of his jaw. The Wyrm cradled the boy's face almost tenderly.

"What are you?" gasped the youth, "What do you want?"

"I am the Wyrm," rasped the creature. "I have to kill you, in the name of my master, the One True Dragon."

The glow in the beast's eyes intensified, and the youth gave a short scream. Crimson rays streamed from the creature's eyes and bathed the shrieking youth. The skin of the young man's face reddened, bubbled white, then turned a smoking black ruin. The scream gave way to a rattling gasp, then silence. The Wyrm held the youth's face, his reddish gaze steady until the blackness itself was charred away to leave only the yellow-white bone beneath.

The Wyrm dropped the boy's body, which slouched wetly against the concrete-block altar. He rubbed a hand over his forehead. Already, the gunshot wounds had been reduced to mere bee-stings, and none of the bodies on the barn floor moved.

The barn around them was fully in flames now, the tongues of fire licking the rafters and the roof. The creature surveyed the damage. The numerous candles had either been toppled in the fight or were melted where they stood into waxen pools. Unaffected by the heat, the winged creature piled some unburned straw on the blaze, encouraging it further.

The Wyrm smiled wearily, a smile filled with serrated fangs. His Master, the True Dragon who protected this world from the Dragons Beyond, would be pleased.

The Wyrm launched itself from the burning pyre of the altar, its huge wings scalloping the superheated air and spreading the fire to the furthest corners of the barn. He left the barn through the entry he had made earlier, itself now a flaming hole in the wall.

He rose on the hot winds of the fire, circling to remain above the barn itself, catching the thermals from the burning youths. The fire was visible on all four sides, framing the black square of the roof in its yellow-orange glow. The paint on the closest pick-up blistered from the heat, and soft plastic parts of the compact began to sag from the nearby flames, but there was little chance of additional explosions, of the fire spreading further.

Pity, thought the Wyrm, considering if it was worth returning to earth and pushing one of the cars into the flames.

Then he heard high-pitched whines and looked away from the burning barn. There was a string of police cars and emergency vehicles already bee-lining towards the barn from the nearest suburb. They were a collection of carnival cars in the darkness, wheeling hubs of blue, white, and red light moving along the road. They were going to arrive faster than the Wyrm had expected.

The Wyrm looked down at the barn beneath him. As he watched, half the roof began to sag and collapse as the supports burned through. It would not matter when they arrived; his job here was finished. Another nest of would-be cultists was crushed. His Master was safe.

The muscles of his wings rippling, the Wyrm turned towards the direction the emergency vehicles came from, back towards the lights of Chicago, to the east. Against the dark, overcast sky, none saw him pass.

Below him, from the wreckage of the barn, a small black cat with green eyes limped away from the flames. It hid itself in the shadow of one of the pick-up's wheels, and slowly, methodically began to lick its scorched paw.

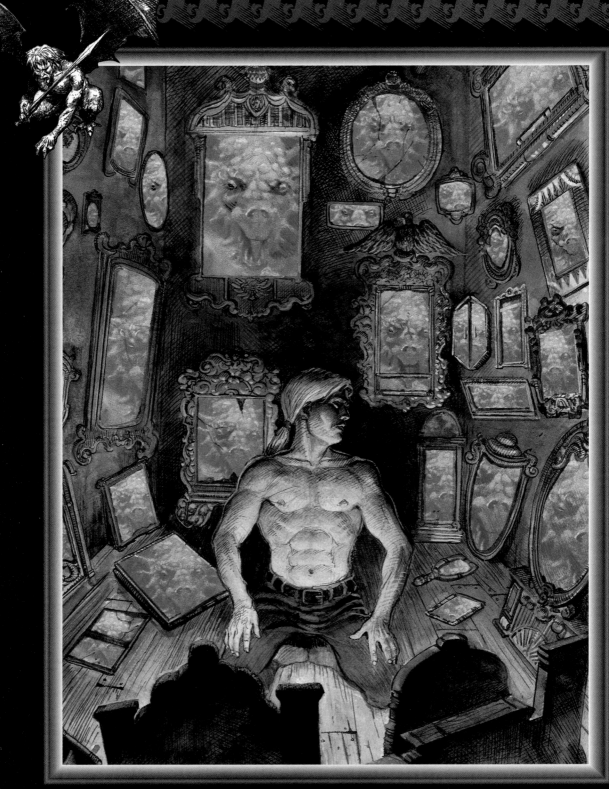

II

⚔ ⚔ ⚔

ARKNESS WAS THE Wyrm's cloak, his protection from upturned eyes that night. He mentally thanked his Master for the boon. Once, long ago, men retired with the sun, and the night hours belonged to the wild things and creatures such as he. Now the darkness below was broken by innumerable smaller lights, stars in their own electrified and civilized constellations, and he had to be more careful.

He flew high over the west Chicago suburbs of Geneva and St. Charles, their lights the soft glow of porch lights and television radiation. As he banked over the brightly-lit arteries of the tollways, each exit was a multi-colored circus of light and activity, the brilliance growing closer together and stronger.

The Wyrm did not feel worried. The chances of his being seen were minimal even on a moonlit night, of being identified more remote, and of being believed reduced to a slight impossibility.

The lights became a milky swirl, a galaxy of illumination, as he flew eastward towards the city over Addison and Bentonville. He might appear as a rogue blip on a radar screen at O'Hare, just to the north. Franklin Park, Elmwood Park, Oak Park, all coagulating light, passed beneath him. The lights were harsher and the buildings taller and more compact as he neared the city.

Once, the sight of the city lights from above amused him, seemed to be a show put on just for his unique vantage. Now he found them tiring. Everything in the modern world seemed tiring to him nowadays.

The private domains of the suburbs now became the clustered shared space of apartment buildings and town houses, and the lights of homes and offices and businesses more common. The electric lifeline of the elevated train whirred beneath him, the ear-ringing clatter of the cars reaching even his ears aloft. The individual neighborhoods now became streets—Cicero, Pulaski, and Kedze. Ahead, the tall concrete and steel mountains of the Loop loomed, beacons against the Lake beyond, their warm illumination bouncing off the clouds above them.

He was not going that far, but rather carefully banked over the decaying buildings of Wicker Park. Long ago, the urban commuters had passed over this neighborhood to more safe and secure locations to the west. They left behind the unwanted—the poor and the minority, the strangely-accented and the struggling, the outrageous and the outcast. The neighborhood's broken-down lofts and former single-family dwellings were now occupied by art students seeking cheap digs, and multiple families unable to afford better. Along Damen Avenue beggars in multiple layers of torn clothes cadged change from shaved-head punks with more silver in their piercings than in their pockets. A few well-heeled yuppies were renovating some of the town-houses, buying their gourmet treats in ethnic groceries whose owners considered such food everyday fare. They were harbingers of an upscale future in a community where most were still struggling just to make the next rent payment.

This was home, for the moment.

The Wyrm circled one three-story building several times, making sure there were no obvious observers. It was a rare occurrence,

few lights on, but nothing out of the ordinary. The third floor was entirely dark.

Folding his wings, The Wyrm dropped silently to the roof's surface. His splayed feet thundered against the hard gravel of the flat roof. Not that he would worry about bothering the tenants below. He was the only occupant of the building's top floor, the only one willing to navigate the rotting stairs to that level.

He padded across the roof to a darkened skylight. The reptilian creature hooked a clawed finger under the skylight edge. It opened easily and almost silently on oiled iron hinges. Somewhere in the world beyond the roof, a distorted guitar grunged in countertime with a blues saxophone. Somewhere further off, a car alarm squealed into the night and the L rattled through the darkness.

The Wyrm turned and dropped through the skylight, entering its lair.

as city-dwellers rarely look up. But the years had made the Wyrm a cautious hunter.

The first floor of the building was an alternative bookstore, selling 'zines, comix, and literature that would not be approved of in a mall bookstore. Its purple-lettered sign hung over the movable gate covering the windows and door. It had shut two hours before, and the store's proprietor, also the landlord, was probably back in his own apartment, curled up with his favorite pipe. The second floor had a

The single main room was large and spartan, occupying half the top floor. In the darkness a second-hand futon and a few mismatched chairs left by the previous owner were laid out in a rough crescent, facing a set of bookcases made of stacked milk cartons. The chairs and bookcases were separated by an upended wooden spool which once carried telephone cable and now served as a low table. A pair of trunks against one wall, both open, with rum-

pled clothes sorted in no apparent order. Two doors, one of which led to the stairs. A low archway which opened into an efficiency kitchen, and beyond it a bathroom stained irrevocably by hard water.

The only part of the room which looked lived in was one corner, where a draftsman's table was propped against the window. The area around the table was littered with sketch-work, discarded curls of paper which glimmered in the dark like ghosts. The draftsman's table was the one sign of life in the otherwise barren surroundings.

The Wyrm settled on the futon, settling into a cross-legged crouch. Slowly, it began to inhale, then exhale, its leathery chest rising and falling in slow, measured strokes, the gunshot wounds nothing more than muscle twinges. The Beast's claws flexed, then relaxed, as the Wyrm let go of the anger within it, let go of the rage which gave him his power, which allowed him to draw upon the Dragon's power.

The conversion was slow but unmistakable, taking a handful of breaths. The flesh began to lighten and grow softer, more supple. The hard pustules and boils which littered his arms and legs shrank to nothing, swallowed by warm, human flesh. The claw-like hands and feet shrank, resembling now mortal hands, though still muscular and hardened by work. The Wyrm's frame also shrank by two feet, reducing him to human dimensions.

The greatest change came in the face. The sharp-toothed muzzle shrank and warped, taking on human form. Finely

carved features, a noble nose, long jaw and sharp cheeks, began to form out of the lizardish flesh. The pebbly skin first became a set of rough scales, its texture like a shirt made of fine chain links, then a set of finer scales, and at last mannish flesh, smooth and unmarked. The white mane of hair remained, though it slid forward on the head, its long tendrils concealing a high forehead. The reddish eyes faded to a gunmetal grey, deeply set beneath a thoughtful brow.

Justin Sterling, the Wyrm, the servant of the True Dragon, took a final deep breath and let it out slowly. He could make the Shifting quicker and easier, but here in his lair he had the time to think, to relax slowly, to shed the rage like savoring a good meal, to enjoy the destruction he had caused. Justin rose and moved through the darkness, flicking on a light switch. His Wyrmform could see in the dark, but not his true self. The bright glow of the unshielded light bulb made everything look flat and even more unattractive. The room did look better in the dark.

Justin rubbed his temples. The night's activity had drained him, more than just a flight and battle should have. He flexed his hands and felt the tired strain of muscles. With the Shifting they had lost the blood spattered on them.

After all these years, he thought, perhaps he was finally feeling his age. Justin padded to the kitchen, pulling a bottle from above the stove. He poured the whiskey into a badly rinsed tumbler, raising it in a mental toast to the cultists he had battled tonight. They were young, and relative innocents in the game between True Dragon and his foes, the Dragons Beyond. But they had played the game, and should be faulted for their failure against a superior foe.

The alcohol burned as it slid down his throat, and warmed him slightly. The exhaustion was deeply ground into his bones, and nothing short of a long sleep would cure it.

The exhaustion was secondary, though, to the feeling of accomplishment that always accompanied a successful mission. The Wyrmform lent strength and vitality to the man. The release of that dark part of himself was comforting—it could go free and battle against his Master's enemies. Then when its bloody job was done, it could be returned and stored away, like the genie into its bottle.

But it never truly went away, of course. There was always a part of Wyrm laying at the base of Justin's brain, coiled around his mind like a serpent, acting as a link between him and his Master. Justin accepted it, as he accepted his long service to the Dragon, the True Dragon. He had lived almost ten times the four-score and ten years ascribed to mortal man, and lived to fight in a great crusade, awaiting his Master's call.

That Master called now, a sharp tug, like a mental leash, secured firmly where Justin's brain met his spinal cord. A siren call, a demand, a summons. Obediently, Justin turned to the other door in the room, the one without numerous locks and chains on it. This once led into a smaller room which was once a walk-in closet.

Justin had refitted the room to his needs. The walls were covered with mirrors of all sizes and shapes; round dresser-mirrors which had been popped from their frames and square portrait-mirrors, tall pier-glass, and swiveled cheval-glass mirrors broken loose of their moorings. Small personal vanities and rear-view mirrors from half a hundred cars. A few fun-house mirrors, convex and concave and plane, throwing back distorted images. One ancient mirror, made by the Saracens of Syria over half a millennium ago. Steel and glass and silver-backed mirrors of every description. All manner of mirrors, all perfectly polished, all mounted on every surface in the small, windowless room.

Justin sat cross-legged in the center of the room and lit a single candle, a thick, worn stump of light that spattered reddish wax across the wooden floor. The flicker caught and rebounded again and again in the room, creating innumerable images of the dancing light.

With the light went Justin's face, framed in a hundred different mirrors from a hundred different angles. Deep-set eyes and sharp, almost crystalline features stared back at the white-haired man. Justin took a deep breath, and opened himself up fully to the Dragon.

The serpent-thing at the base of Justin's brain slithered at the first touch of his master, caressing that brutal, lizard-part of his mind. It caressed the part that dares one to make the swing at a blowhard, to kick a yapping dog, to take that step out over the edge of the chasm. As Justin opened himself up to his Master, he felt that part of his mind stir in response. He closed his eyes to the warmth that issued from the base of his brain.

When he opened them again, there was another face in the reflective mirrors, superimposed over his own.

The face, if face it was, was dark and serpentine, a long neck and snout that shifted and coiled as if made of smoke. Its eyes were Wyrm-red and cat-curious. They held an almost-amused expression.

"Greetings, Sir Justinian. Earl of Sterling," said the Dragon's voice. It seemed to speak aloud, though Justin knew it issued from that dark part of Justin's mind, and could be heard only by him, *"Have you done my bidding this evening?"*

Justin nodded forwards in his seated position. "I have, my lord. The Cultists of the Those Beyond have been eliminated, as you are no doubt aware. They have been slain to a man, and their temple burned to the ground."

The smoke-colored dragon chuckled and Justin felt a warmth in his belly more satisfying than any alcohol. *"You are the finest of my servants, Justinian, the first among equals who work in my name."*

Justin nodded again at the complement. "I only use the gifts you gave me in your name. But ..."

"But?" said the Dragon, *"There is a 'but' here?"*

"Forgive my question, my lord," said the man aloud, "But these enemies seemed very young. They were not warriors, nor scholars, but merely children."

"Step on the weed before it has the chance to grow," said the Dragon, almost offhandedly. *"These meddlers sought to reinstitute my banished brethren, the Dragons Beyond, the foes of the one True Dragon of Earth. Only by your careful vigilance can humanity be spared their return, and the apocalypse it brings."*

Justin nodded. He knew the Dragon's words as if they had been stitched across his heart. Now, after all this time, there was always some group or another to battle, some threat to defeat. He wondered how long he would be successful in his crusade.

"Do you doubt, my servant?" said the Dragon, feeling his unease.

Justin looked up, wondering how much of his concern was visible to his Master. The Dragon in the mirror, in his mind, gave a small laugh

"No, you are just weary," it chuckled. *"You have fought well and hard, and every battle is vital, every hope must be denied the Dragons Beyond, no matter how slender the reed may seem. Do not doubt, my servant, for doubt is the path to destruction. You are my warrior, my knight, my soldier, my strong right hand. Doubt is for lesser beings, and you have long since stopped being one of those fearful creatures. Take faith in me, and in me alone."*

Justin exhaled and felt the renewed resolve within himself, the small flame of his being supported and encouraged by the Dragon. He was a good soldier, a strong right hand. Those who threaten the Dragon would perish, regardless of their innocent appearance.

"Go, my servant," said the Dragon, *"You have performed most adequately. I will be with you, always."*

With that, the smoky image in the mirror faded. All the mirrors reflected were the image of Justin and the low guttering candle.

Justin rose, and the stiffness of his muscles and the sluggishness of his thoughts banished by the close contact with his Master. He always could feel the call from his Master, but his Master was always strongest around mirrors. He could communicate directly without the mirrors, through that serpent-thing at the base of his mind, where the Wyrm slept. But the contact was limited, less rewarding than viewing his Lord in the mirror.

Justin blew out the candle and left it smoking as he opened the door back into his apartment. The phone rang, a high, tinny warble, as he crossed the room. He stopped to pour himself another whiskey, and leaned over and snatched the phone before the answering machine kicked in.

"Hello!" he said, his voice sounding brighter than he felt at the moment.

"Professor Justin Sterling!" said the voice on the other end. Female, soft but with just a hint of authority in it.

"Speaking."

"Sorry to call so late. This is the McHenry County Sherrif's department. Your name has been given to us as an expert in cult activities."

An expert, indeed, Justin thought, the first true smile crossing his human face, "That's true," he said instead, "How can I help you?"

"We've had an incident west of Geneva," said the voice, and Justin could hear the parenthesis around the word "incident." "It appears to be a situation where your knowledge could be useful. Are you available this evening?"

Justin's smile grew—was he available to investigate a crime he had himself committed? "Tonight? I supposed so. That's farm country out there. Are we dealing with cattle mutilators, or crop circles hoaxers?"

"Something much worse," said the voice on the other end, flat and clearly unamused. "We'll send a car for you."

Justin gave the address and said he would be waiting out front. He cradled the phone quietly and firmly after the woman on the other end disconnected. There was a shadow of something familiar about her voice. Not exact, but similar, like a ghost of the past.

Not that his past didn't have enough ghosts, Justin reflected. But with the Dragon's help, he had kept most of the memories of his past at bay.

He had time to shower and tie his long white hair back in a loose ponytail. He donned a white cotton shirt a half-size too large, well-worn Levis, and his old Doc Martens, purchased in the days before they were popular with the goths and punks. He pulled a suit coat with a grey houndstooth check from his trunk. The night was cool, but more importantly, the suit coat was part of the "visiting expert" look. He folded his long black leather trench coat over his arm.

He looked briefly at the sketches littering the drafting table. Mostly human figure studies, they were bulky and incomplete. Justin promised himself he would get back to them, eventually, but there never seemed to be time.

No rest for the wicked, he thought, heading for the door, *though after 600 years, you'd think I would gain a respite.*

At the base of his brain, the serpent-form slithered and seemed to laugh at the idea.

III

🝔 🝔 🝔

THE FARM WITNESSED A false dawn of emergency and police vehicles. Powerful beacons sliced through the night around the wreckage of the barn, casting confusing shadows across the scorched and blackened earth. The surviving grass surrounding the ruined structure had been mashed flat by tires and booted feet. The barn was a smashed parody of itself, one surviving corner transfixed by the pale, artificial light. The ruins were still smoking and popping, and the fire department was rolling up the last of their yellow hoses as Justin arrived on the scene.

Accompanied by his police escort, Justin circled the barn at a distance. An observer would assume that he was trying to get the big picture before concentrating on any details. Actually, Justin was admiring his handiwork. So often his activities went unrecognized. He had long-since gotten past the point of personal vanity in his actions, but it was good to see someone else was paying attention.

The police driver, a heavy-set Pole with five too many consonants at the start of his name, gave him the known details on the way out. Someone had spotted the fire from the road and called it in on their cellular phone. By the time they arrived, the barn had already gone up like kindling. They moved the cars back and tried to find any survivors, but that was impossible until the flames had been doused. They pulled ten, maybe a dozen bodies out, said the driver, repeating what others had told him. The bodies were dressed in long robes and there were some markings on some of the surviving wood that indicated cult activity.

Someone asked someone else who would be around and able to give advice *muy pronto*, and Sterling's name came up. The driver also grunted something insincere about getting him up at this late hour.

Justin made the appropriate noises about how it was no problem at all, he got his best work done at night. Inwardly, he smiled—the beginning was always the best time to quash any ideas of cult theories, to put the reins on any theories of darker powers at work. It had been years since anyone had even started to suspect his not-so-gentle hand in such matters, in part due to his own willingness to guide the investigations in other directions. Justin was very good at what he did.

Justin also made a note that cell-phones would increase reaction time from the authorities, pitching the thought towards the part where the Wyrm dwelled. The serpent in his mind did not respond, but lay coiled at the base of his brain like a kitten by the fire. It would uncurl only at his Master's will.

The bodies had apparently been removed from the scene, their locations marked with white tape outlines, reverse silhouettes against the ash. Justin moved through the ruined barn now, careful to keep back from the police searching the ash. One in particular, a blonde woman with her hair pulled back in a bun, was in intense discussion with one of the uniforms. She was kneeling and pointing out something among the unburned refuse.

"Lieutenant!" said the driver "The cult expert is here."

The woman rose and turned. She was dressed sensibly but not elegantly—loose slacks and a blouse with a dark leather vest.

Her face was wide, her eyes sky blue and intensely intelligent. Her hair was not just blonde, but cornflower blonde.

Another face, one long ago forgotten, swam in front of Justin's eyes for a moment, then faded. The face of a woman dead for almost 600 years. Justin stared for a moment, and the woman repeated her question.

"Professor Sterling?" said the woman again, her brows slightly knitted in concern. Hers was the voice on phone, steel wrapped in velvet.

"I'm sorry," said the man, recovering his poise, "Yes, I'm Justin Sterling. I came as soon as I could. Your man gave me the basics about what happened here."

"Nasty work," said the woman, holding out a hand, "Detective Lieutenant Stone. I appreciate you coming out."

"My pleasure," said Justin, taking the hand briefly. Another memory of another touch played across the back of his brain. Justin frowned slightly, then pressed on, "What do you have here?"

Lt. Stone sighed, "Happened just about midnight. Eight bodies, most of them burned beyond recognition. Dressed in some kind of loose robes. Weird markings on some of the boards. Lots of candles and incense in the barn. Some material that looks ritual in nature. I wanted to get an expert in before somebody says anything at a press conference."

Justin kneeled next to the plank Lt. Stone had been investigating. It was the surface of the plywood top of the altar. The edges buckled and oozed from the heat, but the symbology was still there, still scuffed by his earlier landing as the Wyrm.

"The bodies were in robes?" said Justin, looking at the scribbled marks as if they were inscriptions in the Rosetta Stone. "What were they wearing underneath?"

The lieutenant looked at the other officer, then shrugged, "Streets. Jeans, T-shirts, and sneakers. Nothing unusual."

"Age?"

"College age," said the female officer, "We won't know for sure until the bodies are identified, but they look young. Freshmen class, maybe Sophomores."

"Hmmmm," said Justin, who looked out into the middle distances as if trying to make everything fit.

Lt. Stone added, "We also found some equipment that might be ritual in nature: A mirror, a cage, some animal material."

"Skull?" said Justin, "Maybe a snake's skin?"

Lt Stone nodded, "Of course, that might just have been in the barn before. It hasn't been used for years, now."

"Hmmmmpf," said Justin, looking at the woman. She stood tall and proud, unbowed by responsibility or pressure. The face, the voice, the way she stands. This one was so reminiscent of his Gwendolyne.

Justin blinked. It had been the first time since the Twenties he had thought of his wife's name.

Stone noticed his distraction, "You have something?"

"Really too soon to tell," said the self-proclaimed

expert, "You'll probably find that your so-called cultists are teenagers, probably from good families, probably some are in colleges. You find alcohol or drugs?"

"A hip-bottle of aquavit," said the lieutenant, pushing an errant strand of blonde hair out of her eyes, "A lot of beer cans and bottles. Rolling Rock and Miller. More empties, of the same brands, in the bed of one of the pick-up trucks."

"Uh-huh," said Sterling, allowing his face to broaden in a wide smile, "I'm glad you called me, Lieutenant. I think there was a ceremony here this evening, but it had as much to do with legitimate cult activity as Bingo does with organized religion."

He looked at the uniformed officer with the lieutenant and saw the relief spread across the uniform's wide face. That one was just looking for the excuse to write off this tragedy as an accident, as a mistake, as anything else than what it seemed to be.

"You think this is not a real cult?" said the lieutenant, her face still tight and concerned.

"Not as you probably mean it, and not as you should think of a cult. This was likely a group of kids who saw something or read something and figured that a little midnight ceremony would jazz up a Friday night beer blast. Their 'high priest' was probably an economics major who bought a copy of the *Necronomicon* at Half-Price Books. The stupid things that kids do, but kids do it all the time. Until something like this happens. Until something goes horribly awry."

The lieutenant nodded, but nodded slowly, still thinking of Justin's words. The uniformed officer was nodding more quickly and enthusiastically. Justin had sold that one. A strong initial refuting would keep the newshounds at bay. Sterling looked around, and noted for the first time that there were no news wagons in the area. They were far west of the Chicago suburbs. As soon as this became housing developments, something like this would be part of the regular coverage on the ten o'clock news, with newsreaders "live on the scene" looking earnest and serious for their home viewing audience.

"What probably happened," Justin tried to look thoughtful, "Is that one of the boys thought it would be a cool thing to hold a sacrifice. Call up the devil, or the spirit of Ed Gein, or whatever. He and his friends get loaded, dress up in badly-tailored bedsheets and pass out some mumbo-jumbo they got watching the Son of Svengoolie on channel nine. In the middle of everything, somebody drops a candle in the straw, and the building goes up. The boys die in the panic to get out."

"Possible," Stone looked at the uniform, and added, "Likely. We did find some nasty wounds on the bodies. They looked chewed up pretty bad, even with the burns."

"We're in the country," Justin blandly stated the obvious, "Wild animals? Dogs?"

"No time," said the lieutenant, shoving back another piece of hair. "We had to put the fire out, and it looks like the boys died in the fire—we'll know more after the autopsies."

Justin was silent for a moment, thinking the fire should have been more effective than it was. "Falling beams, then. Rusted nails and fixtures. Could they have created some of those wounds?"

"Again, possible," said the blonde woman, "They were really badly messed up, and the roof collapsing on them didn't do any good. We also found this."

She hefted the pick-headed axe, the one with the large narrow triangle of what looked like yellow-white stone. The handle had been blackened in the fire, but the scorched rawhide lashing held the head firm.

Justin was surprised. He had not seen such a device when he burst into the the barn and cut down the fools like sheep. Where had this been?

Simultaneously he realized what the blade of the axe was. It was the tooth of a Dragon. Like the Dragons Beyond. Like his Master.

His look of surprise was not lost on the police lieutenant. "You recognize this?"

"No," said Justin, then added, "Maybe. It's not the type of thing you find at your standard beer-bash." He rubbed his thumb over the inside curve of the tooth. Sharp as the day it was pulled from the dragon's mouth. "Any blood on it?"

Lt. Stone shook her head.

Justin examined the device carefully and agreed with the female detective. Even with his mortal vision he could see that this item had not been used. If he had known, he would have used it instead of his own claws. It would have made things much simpler.

"Intriguing," he said at length, "A murder weapon without a murder." He handed the picked-headed axe back to the Lieutenant.

"You know something about this," said the woman.

Not a question, but a fact. This woman had fire in her heart, Justin thought. She could see into people, and cut away the excess dross, like Gwendolyne did.

Justin Sterling nodded, then shrugged, "I think so. It may require some explaining. Can we go somewhere?"

"In a minute," she said, "We have to wrap this up."

In a minute meant in another hour, as the police photographers took the last of their shots and the uniforms decked the area in festive yellow tape. There would be more in the morning, and officers would remain on the site for a while.

During the hour, Justin Sterling leaned against one of the fire-darkened trucks, wondering at his own behavior. He had practiced his stories many times, growing with his practice to the point that he could fool a lie detector. Yet he had been caught off-guard by the appearance of the Dragon's Tooth. Perhaps he was getting old.

And the appearance of the Lieutenant herself. With her hair down, in ringlets, she could be Gwendolyne, his wife. Sweet Gwen, dying Gwen, Gwen turned mad and rotted by the plague. Her voice and stance, the way she pushed the hair out of her eyes, the color of her eyes.

At the base of his brain, the Wyrm stirred. It felt like two pieces of slate grinding against each other.

No, it was just the late hour, and the surprise of the Dragonstooth Blade. His resolve was steady, his faith in the True Dragon unchanged and unchallenged. The unease at the base of his brain returned to its dark sleep.

Still, he was waiting for her, when he could easily slip away with an excuse and a phone number to be called later.

Lt. Stone strode up, refastening her hair back in a new bun as she talked, "Done here. Coffee? I've got wheels."

"Wheels" turned out to be a Jeep Cherokee with four-wheel drive parked on the road embankment. Deep green with slate-grey interior, a car phone mounted next to the gear shift. Cleaned recently, but not well—a few stale french fries crunched under Justin's heels.

There was a diner down the road towards Geneva, one of those long, low ones with a non-franchised name and trucks parked on the gravel in the back. Wide windows opened out on the empty streets and dark buildings. A few patrons were visible seated at the counter.

"Looks like a Edward Hopper painting," said Justin as the policewoman parked in front.

"Right, *Night Owls*," said the lieutenant.

"*Nighthawks*," corrected Justin, "They have it hanging down at the Art Institute. Night owls are fools who stay up when wise people are busy sleeping off the previous day."

"The graveyard shift is pretty rewarding," said Stone, climbing out of her side of the Jeep, "Until it becomes a real graveyard."

The waitress waved a friendly hello as they entered, and Stone called her by name.

They grabbed a booth and the waitress approached, coffee pot in hand, a pair of cups hooked onto her fingers. Justin drank his black. Lt. Stone took two creams in hers.

"So tell me about the dingus," said Stone.

"Not much to tell," said Justin, "I was surprised to see it. It's the only thing in the equation that runs against the pattern."

"Pattern?"

Justin rubbed his hands together over his cup, as if for warmth. "Cult activities, real cult activities, usually have more of a motivation. An ultimate goal, whether it's bilking believers of their worldly possessions, setting up some ultimate retreat from the wicked world, or even planning for some apocalypse."

"Jim Jones," said the policewoman.

"Correct," continued Justin, acting very much like the professor he claimed to be, "What you have here is just a group of kids playing Meet the Devil. Without the fire, they would have just gotten drunk and hauled themselves home at a late hour. Real cultists, the ones who think in terms of poison Kool-Aid, don't work like that. They need artifacts to give themselves some sense of legitimacy. Artifacts like this 'dingus.' Even with it, it's probably just kids playing, but I wonder where they got it in the first place."

Stone looked at him over the lip of her mug for long time. "You're not what I expected, Professor Sterling," she said at last.

"Justin, please," he said with a tired smile, "What do you mean, Lieutenant Stone?"

"Alexandra, or Alex, or just Al," she replied, "Most 'cult experts' are quick to find evil influence everywhere and in everything. And aren't shy about talking about it, particularly to the media. You seem unwilling to find the devil here. I find that curious."

Justin gave a theatrical sigh. "A lot of your 'cult experts' are looking for their next big score, their next book and their next talk show tour. They fearlessly sound the alarm when there is no danger, in order to paint themselves as protectors. Were I one of that type I would have brought the papers with me. I'm not. I've helped local law enforcement groups before, and that's probably why someone gave you my name. I know my business, and how to keep quiet."

And, he added to himself, how to cover his own tracks effectively. Keep tempers cool, threats unuttered.

Lt. Alexandra Stone regarded him with the wide, blue eyes, "British," she said at last.

Justin nodded. "Its been many years, but yes. I'm told I still have a bit of an accent, particularly when I'm lecturing. The family was landed nobility, many, many generations ago."

Stone smiled and set her empty mug down. The waitress manifested immediately with a fresh pot in hand. "So, what about the dingus," she said again.

"It's odd because it doesn't belong here," said Justin, "It belongs to another set of cults entirely, real cults with monasteries and holy men and books of lore. Hardly the kind of thing that some college kid is going to find on the street."

Justin spread his long thin fingers out as if conjuring an image. "The axe is called a Dragonstooth Blade. It's usually made with a fossilized dinosaur tooth, though I've seen ones made of walrus ivory or shards of obsidian. It's supposed to hold the power of the legendary Dragons. You know about dragons?"

"Movies," said Alexandra Stone, "TV and stuff. Saint George and all that. They seem to be everywhere nowadays, like cute unicorns."

"Modern echoes of a distant past," said Justin, "The Dragon has always represented the darker side of nature, the cunning beast, the tempter and in more recent times, the devil."

"This item," he said, tapping the formica table top for effect, "Rightly belongs with an Eastern group known as Drokpas, or Dragon People. They are a real cult, not some gathering of students or con-artists, seeking a quick buck, though nothing has been heard of them for over a century.

"Drokpa thinking says that there were once two breeds of Dragon, Eastern and Western. They say that, in the dim prehistory, man and dragon battled for control of the land. The dragons ruled the Earth, and man rebelled against that rule. The Eastern Dragons were driven away from the Earth itself, into another mystic land, where they gained the name of the Dragons Beyond. The mightiest of the Western Dragons, the True Dragon, befriended man, and served as a guardian of the gates between this world and the next. This Dragon supposedly stands between the two worlds, as a protector. The Drokpas supposedly sought to return the Dragons Beyond to this plane, which would bring about the end of the world. The Disciples of the True Dragon sought to prevent it."

"Hmmmm," said the lieutenant. "Who won?"

Justin let out a tired laugh, "Well, we're still here, so I suppose the True Dragon is still protecting the Earth. Both cults seemed to peter out after a while, subsumed by other beliefs and other rituals. There was a resurgence in England at the end of the last century, at a time when all things Eastern were considered exciting and exotic. The largest group rivaled the Order of the Golden Dawn itself. Like the Golden Dawn, these renovated Dragon People fell to internal politics and not a few mysterious fires." He shrugged, as if entertaining a new thought, "Perhaps the same thing happened here. Maybe there was an alcohol-

fueled argument that started the fire that destroyed them all. That might account for the additional damage."

"We found a gun with empty chambers," said Alexandra, "but no bullet wounds on the bodies."

The policewoman loosened the bun of cornflower hair, and pushed the loose strands back, then swore mildly. "Excuse me," she said, pulling the band from her hair and retying it in a neat ponytail to match Justin's own.

Justin watched her intently in this simple action. The policewoman seemed like a reverberation of Gwendolyne's personality, brought into the present day.

Justin continued, "The Dragonstooth Blade was a tool of the Drokpas, the followers of the Dragons Beyond. Used as a ritual device, though not for sacrifice. Rather the temple guardians used it as a badge of honor, a supposedly historical weapon that defeated some nasty beast in the past. Legend says that the True Dragon and his followers could be slain by such weapons, which had a bit of a dragon or a holy man contained in the making. I'm no expert on this part, but this one looked like a fossilized dinosaur tooth"

"So one faction is the Drokpas, the followers of these Dragons Beyond. What about the followers of the True Dragon, the guardian?"

Justin paused for a moment, then said, "Where I have seen references to the True Dragon's disciples, they are called Little Dragons. Wyrms, if you would."

"Worms?"

"Wyrms with a 'Y'," said Justin, "Supposedly a flightless variety of dragon, though it all gets mixed up in mythology. Several of the Dragons of England were well and truly Wyrms."

"In any event," he said, stretching out on the bench seat of the booth, "Earlier I said something about one of the youths getting hold of an occult book in a used-book store."

"*Necronomicon* in a Half-Price Books," corrected Alexandra. Justin nodded in agreement.

"This old item may be the trigger that set it off, that caused the interest in the first place. A device from a forgotten ritual, a little mumbo-jumbo, and the first thing you know they try to set themselves up as cultists of the beer-god. Nothing else really ties in specifically with the Drokpas or their cult."

"Come on, gang, there's an old barn out back. Let's summon a demon!" said the woman, and laughed. It was a pleasant laugh.

Justin smiled easily, "Exactly. I'm sorry for the youths, but this is more an accident than a homicide, and the youths dead of their own foolishness more than any arcane force. 'Death by misadventure' is what they call it in England.

Pity you don't have a similar term here."

Alexandra Stone tapped her cup with a fingernail. "We may find out where they got it when the survivor wakes up."

Justin almost choked on his coffee, "Survivor?" he managed.

The lieutenant nodded, not seeming to notice Justin's reaction. "There was a breather in the pack. Really badly burned, and his guts ripped open, his neck snapped, a real mess, but still breathing. He managed to haul himself outside before the roof came in. He's in ICU at Saint Vinnie's, now. Outside shot he might make it."

"Interesting," said Justin, his eyes becoming slits, admiring how the policewoman pulled all the information from him before playing this last card. At the base of his mind, the Wyrm slowly uncoiled and seemed to yawn in displeasure. "I'd like to talk to him."

Alexandra Stone managed a dark smile, "So would we. The EMTs said he was screaming about demons. Which is why we called you in the first place."

Witnesses are not allowed, hissed the lizard-like voice in the back of Justin's brain, and he felt the familiar tug of his Master's leash. *Kill the boy*, it said.

"Interesting," repeated Justin, "This has been a most intriguing evening. I wish we had met in more pleasant circumstances."

Lt. Stone gave him a warm smile, "Me too."

The Dragon repeated silently in the depths of Justin's brain, *Kill the Boy. No witnesses. He must die.* The connection was weaker than that in front of the mirror, but still strong. Justin knew that the link was weaker away from the mirrors. It cost the True Dragon more energy to communicate at a distance.

All in good time, said Justin mentally, *I have to finish my coffee.*

For the rest of the early morning, until Alexandra dropped Justin off at the bookstore, the serpent-like voice at the base of Justin Sterling's brain remained silent, as if it were sulking.

IV

ST. VINCENT'S WAS towards the city, a short ride on the L from Wicker Park. The Dragon had given him time to fetch a gym bag containing an old tape recorder from his apartment. A phone call netted the survivor's room number, but only after Justin invoked Lt. Stone's name.

The nearly-empty rail car swayed and rattled through the early hours of the morning like a spastic cradle. It was awfully close to morning, and Justin would have preferred to wait for the next evening, in the depths of the night. But his master had been insistent; the survivor must be taken care of before he could speak of the Wyrm's presence at the barn.

It made good sense, but Justin was tired. He tried to concentrate on the subject at hand, remember what he knew of the area. The original teaching hospital had sprawled through adjacent buildings to form a full-fledged health complex of offices, labs, and private rooms. Good care facilities, but in the heart of a bad part of the city. A lot of abandoned buildings in the area, waiting for the wrecking ball and new expansions of the complex.

But Justin's attention kept wandering, coming back to the police lieutenant, back to Alexandra Stone. The sharpness of her features, the openness of her clean blue eyes, the apparent silky softness of her blonde hair. Surely it would feel the same if he touched it, feel just the same as...

Justin frowned as another face swam upwards, one buried for so many decades. Sometimes it would take the smell of horses, or a piece of music performed on archaic instruments, or some old reading that would take him back. But this time, she seemed so close. More importantly, she seemed as wise as Gwendolyne had been. Wise and funny and sweet. Until the madness and the pox took her.

The Dragon flexed and spoke to him from the base of his brain. *I saved you,* it said, its voice small but only slightly apologetic, *and I would have saved your wife, if I could. But she was too far gone, the madness of the plague had taken her. She could not open herself to the darkness in the mirror. She did not have the strength.*

And here she was again, thought Justin. Not the same woman, but similar, the random factors of genetics combining into a doppleganger. This Alexandra Stone seemed stronger, more determined, more independent than any woman could have been in his mortal time. She was not Gwendolyne, but a shadow of the past, a doppleganger.

A doppleganger who was willing to spend an hour with him at a run-down diner outside Geneva, Illinois, talking artifacts and cults.

The L car shifted sharply on the tracks and rocked Justin back to the present. They were almost at the stop for St. Vinnie's. The images of Alexandra and of Gwen were ripped away like morning clouds. It was time for business, now.

The streets were still empty at this hour, the graveyard shift having a few more hours to run. Justin padded down the empty streets, ducking into an alleyway among boarded-up houses sprayed with ancient gang graffiti. The alley was a dead end, a wire fence covered with wooden boards blocking the other end, overturned trash bins on either side. It had been years since garbage trucks had made regular stops here.

Justin stepped behind one of the bins and stripped quietly and efficiently, as he had innumerable times before, a preparation to go into battle. Each garment was carefully folded and placed in the bag, alongside the tape recorder. Justin took a deep breath and began the Shifting.

Deep in the heart of every man's soul is that part that, confronted with a cliff's edge, desires to take the final step. That when confronted with a whirling blade, wants to hold out their hand. That when gripping a gun, lusts to pull the trigger. That is the home of the Dragon. Justin went to that place, that edge, and confidently stepped off, into the void beyond.

The transformation came quickly, as it always did in these later days. His flesh swelled and became leathery, with bulbous patches reminiscent of the the plague that had almost claimed him. The sinews of his arms toughened and grew, straining like steel cables beneath this new flesh. From his shoulder blades erupted spurs of bone, which soon were draped in the thick fold of wing-flesh. His legs elongated and bent backwards, the weight resting on splayed, claw-hooked toes. His face lengthened, his mouth filled with teeth like steak-knives. His eyes shifted from slate grey to red, pupiless orbs, glowing of their own hatred. The only thing that remained unchanged was his silver-grey hair, now dangling on all sides of his reptilian skull like a tangle of metal wire.

The shifting took less than ten seconds.

There was a sharp intake of breath elsewhere in the alley, and a curse in Spanish.

Justin might have missed it, but the Wyrm missed nothing. It wheeled and tore through the back of the alley, overturning garbage cans to get to the heart of the sound.

It was a young woman with short multi-colored hair closely cropped to her skull, her eyes rheumy, her tattooed skin sallow, dressed in ragged jeans and tank shirt too light for the weather. At her feet was a junkie's rig—spoon, vial, light, hose, and hypodermic, all in an open leather case. She was trying to crab walk backwards, away from her toys, and away from the Wyrm.

The Wyrm didn't give her time to scream. He gripped her by the face with one powerful hand and slammed her against the brick wall behind her. She made a gurgling, crying noise and he slammed her again, then again, until her skull started to make mushy noises against the brick and left a dark stain against the graffiti. Only then did he let go, letting her slide wetly down the wall.

Sloppy in your old age, said the chuckling voice at the base of his brain. The Wyrm made no reply. Instead he zipped up the junkie's case and slipped it into the gym bag, and launched himself into the the morning darkness.

Beyond the lights of the Loop, the sky was already starting to lighten from black to deep blue.

St. Vinnie's was a maze of interlocked buildings, but he knew Intensive Care was on the fifth floor of the largest and oldest of the buildings, a brick monstrosity with wide ledges ringing the floors. According to the voice on the phone, the survivor had been moved to a semi-private room on the same floor. Someone had spent money to keep the kid alive.

The Wyrm moved with cat-like grace along the outside of the building, checking two darkened and empty rooms before finding the one with the survivor. From the window he could see the boy wired up to enough machinery to launch a communications satellite.

The Wyrm hefted at the window and it rose a half-inch, then froze in position, secured from within. With a smile and a grunt, Justin pushed at the top of the frame and with a sharp snap, the window slid all the way up. He waited for a moment to see if his actions brought any of the nurses. Then, folding his wings, he slid into the room.

The boy should not have survived, would not have survived such an attack even ten years ago. Both arms were in casts, and his torso and chest were swaddled in white bandages, topped by a huge collar holding his head in place. Breathing tubes ran into the boy's nose and throat.

The Wyrm saw a hint of moustache under the tubing. The survivor was the one who shot him. The wounds were immaterial now, but the monster touched his chest at the memory of the bullets.

The room was silent except for the soft humming of the monitors. Justin could not identify half of them, and wondered briefly at the changes in medicine since the last time he was a surgeon. He loomed over the boy, and pulled the junkie's rig out of the gym bag.

The boys eyes opened. Not fluttered, like someone coming out of a sleep, or snapped open in terror. Just opened. Blanketed by medication, they held no fear.

"You Danjel," said the boy through the tubes.

"Danger?" said the Wyrm, following one tube to the saline jar it came from with a curved talon. He reached down with his other hand and turned on the tape recorder.

"Da Anjel uh Deaf." said the boy slowly. The angel of death.

The Wyrm said nothing. The boy made no move to the nurse's button, but some of the graphs began to hop and sputter, pale yellow on kelp-green screens.

"Sorry," said the boy, fighting to get the words out. "Godime sorry. Dint know. Jayce idea. Dint know."

"Jay's idea," repeated the Wyrm, its voice a harsh whisper. "What was Jay's idea?"

The boy said nothing understandable. The Wyrm unzipped the junkie's rig, pulling out the white vial and spoon.

"What was Jay's idea?" repeated the Wyrm, "Where did he get the axe?"

"Godime so sorry. Dint know."

"The axe," said the Wyrm, "Where did he get the axe?" He shook out as much of the vial as the spoon would hold. His eyes flashed red, and the crystals melted into a sticky pool at the base of the spoon.

"Prafess at yousee," said the boy. Professor at the University of Chicago. "Tuk it fum him. Stolit. Sorry, Godime sorry."

"Which Professor?" said the Wyrm, loading the needle, sucking all of the pure drug into the syringe. He put the spoon back into the kit and rezipped it, putting the entire rig, except for the needle, back into the gym bag.

"Prafess Dunkle," said the boy. His eyes began to water as the Wyrm held the needle up, squirting a bit of the fluid out of the tip. The boy made a half-hearted attempt to rise, but the combination of bandages, casts, and medication was too much for him.

"Dugan?" said the Wyrm calmly, placing the needle's tip against the saline feed. With the other hand he pinched the tube. He depressed the plunger, shooting the smack into the feed.

"Dun," said the boy, "Kan." Tears were beginning to flow down the side of his face. The mammalian part of his brain, the reasoning center, was finally kicking in, realizing what would happen. "Goddam imesorry, pleez don hur me, Danjel. Pleez."

Duncan. Professor Duncan at UC. The Wyrm smiled and relaxed his hold on the saline feed. The drug-filled liquid resumed its flow into the boy.

The reaction was immediate, faster than Justin had anticipated, the smack coursing into the boy's system with a lethal rush. The pale yellow lines now zig-zagged across the screen, and one of the machines began to make a frantic beeping noise.

The Wyrm had to hurry now. He snagged the gym bag with one hand, and scooped up the boy with both arms. He cradled the youth like a child and rushed for the window. Monitor leads lengthened behind them and pulled from their sockets. Another machine made a ratcheting screech behind him. In a few moments the nurses would burst into the room, alerted by their own monitors.

The Wyrm threw the boy out the window, then lofted himself out of the building in the next second.

The Wyrm beat his wings and rose. The boy spread his plastic-encased arms and plummeted, his body spiraling against the dark concrete below until he struck. He did not bounce.

The Wyrm struggled upwards quickly, as nothing draws eyes upwards faster than a falling body. He cleared the office wing of St. Vincent's, circled once, and returned to the alleyway where he changed before. This time he checked for other occupants, but there was no one present save for the girl with the crushed skull.

The Wyrm gathered himself together and sat in the filth of the alleyway, behind the trash bin. Spurred by haste and necessity, the shifting back took less time than otherwise, and small pains laced through his joints as his body returned to human form. In the space of three deep breaths the Wyrm had been returned to its place within him. He dressed quickly and returned the junkie's rig to her, laying it open on her lap.

Justin stepped out of the alleyway. A young man with a mohawk and black combat pants, carrying an artist's portfolio, gave him the fish-eye, but Justin just smiled and passed him by, making for the hospital.

It took all of five minutes, and it was like he had stirred up a nest of ants. Police were swarmed around the front entrance, along one side. The requisite yellow tape had already been deployed. Beacons of white, red, and blue light from the cars cascaded against the dark brick facade.

Justin waded through the mass of people, too many for the early morning hour. A nervous fat woman was manning the front desk, her eyes locked on the main entrance. Justin put on his best smile and asked if he could see someone about interviewing a patient.

The nervous fat woman snapped the regular visiting hours at him, her eyes never leaving the front door.

"I need to see someone who is in ICU," said Justin, trying to sound patient and confused and British and refined. "Brought in this morning. It's rather important, I fear. Is there a doctor or nurse I can talk to..."

"You're too late," said a familiar voice behind him. "We lost him."

Justin turned, eyebrows raised, to see Lt. Alexandra Stone. The errant strand of blonde hair had gotten loose again, now joined by several others, and her blue eyes were now rimmed with the first touch of red. Justin smiled, then looked at her, puzzled, "Lost him! He died!"

Alexandra shrugged her shoulders in a disgusted fashion. "Leaper. Took a header off the fifth floor. They still haven't brought him in. Healthy guy wouldn't survive that plunge. This one..." she shrugged again.

"I'm sorry," said Justin, "I thought I could talk to him, find out where the axe came from. I thought..."

Alexandra shook her head, "Ditto. It looks like both of us got here too late. Look, it's going to be a zoo here for a while. You go home, and I'll call you when we have anything."

"If you need any help..." started Justin.

"Go. Home." said the Lieutenant, shifting into cop-voice, then softening slightly. "I'll call. We'll do the meal-thing when I have something. OK! Its been a busy night, and it's not going to stop."

Justin managed a small embarrassed blush and stepped back towards the doors, "OK. I will await your call."

Alexandra gave a small wave and turned to the overweight nurse, rapid-firing a series of questions. Justin didn't know what Alexandra said, but the fat woman looked at the police officer, not at the door. It was as if Justin had suddenly been swallowed up by the darkness outside and forgotten.

Some might feel irritated by that. Justin walked back to the Metra station, whistling softly. Behind him the first light of dawn was painting the upper floors of the surrounding buildings.

It had been a busy night, indeed.

V

IS MASTER WAS pleased with the news, both that the survivor was dead, and that the origin of the axe had been discovered. Justin always felt the Dragon near him, but the connection was tenuous away from the mirror, at best, sound without picture. There was only a shadow of the great beast's power when they were apart, only a fraction of the majesty found in the Hall of Mirrors.

Justin slept for most of the day. It had been years since the Wyrm could fly easily and unchallenged in daylight, and Justin had shifted his energies accordingly. He had become a nighthawk, a night owl, one of the people of the dark hours when the rest of the world slumbered without knowing what truly occurred when they were asleep.

He woke briefly, only to affirm the existence of a Cyrus Duncan, Guest Professor at U of C in Cultural Anthro, then napped for the rest of the day. The Dragon, tickling the back of his brain, like an unforgiving alarm clock, woke him at sundown.

Justin considering briefly going in human form, to lure out the good Professor, find out how much he knew of the Dragonstooth Blade, then Shifting into Wyrmform at the last moment, giving the man a heart attack along with a validation of his work, that yes, Dragons did exist.

He shook his head, and decided against it for two reasons. First, he had no real explanation for going there other than the words of a dying boy, a boy he killed. Secondly, his regular appearance at multiple homicides would attract the attention of even the dullest of the police and media. And Lt. Stone was no dullard.

This would have to be done entirely as the Wyrm, regardless of the risk.

Professor Duncan lived in Wrigleyville, the haven of Cub fans surrounding the park. Its main avenues were crammed chockablock with all manner of restaurants, shops, and taverns. Particularly taverns. But as soon as

one turned onto a side street, the bright lights dropped away, and the area was dominated by renovated town houses and apartment complexes, almost overgrown with ancient trees, oaks dating back to the before the Great Fire. Rounding a corner onto one of those streets is like traveling into a different universe, as the thick vegetation screened out the city, the noise, and most importantly, the light.

Justin was counting on the cover of the trees as he sailed high above the city. The night was mild that evening, and partly cloudy, and there was the small but real danger of being spotted. Against the night sky, it was hard to determine size, so if seen, the viewer might assume that it was some smaller creature flapping though the night. Sometimes, in other places, he had grown careless over time. There had been multiple spottings, until they became too numerous to ignore, and he had to move on.

Wrigley Field was a volcano of light. After years of day games and tradition, they finally installed huge banks of stadium lighting, creating a radiant beacon that reflected off the natural grass and leaped skyward in an explosion of brilliance. There were crowd noises from within the ballpark. The Cubs were playing at home.

The professor's apartment building was three blocks west of the field. The Wyrm folded his wings and dropped

sharply, spreading them only at the last moment to land softly on the building's roof. The apartment building was four stories high, and Duncan had his quarters on the third floor.

To the east, there was the sharp, staccato pop of wood striking horsehide, and the bellows of the crowd rising to its feet. Silently the Wyrm moved down the scaffolding of the fire escape. It was a pleasant night, and there were numerous windows open. The Wyrm took care not to cross in front of any lit windows.

The professor's window was open as well, the light from within soft and inviting. The old man was crouched over his desk facing away from the window, speaking intently on the phone. He was an ancient man, dressed indifferently, a dirty white sweater vest covering a T-shirt of indeterminate color, slacks of a neutral shade.

A single ceiling lamp illuminated the room with a sickly yellow glow. The room itself was decorated in a style known as Academic Disaster Area. Books and loose papers were stacked on every available flat surface. Justin noted some of the titles. Some were in his own collection. One or two were by Justin himself. What parts of the room not swallowed by the paper maelstrom were given over to baseball memorabilia. Pennants with cartoon bears, grizzly heads, and large capital Cs were thumbtacked into the walls.

A couple of signed bats were stuck into a wire basket. A desk radio was on, but turned down, the announcer's voice a distant ant. Professor Duncan fiddled with a signed baseball as he spoke.

The Wyrm froze by the window, but the professor kept on talking, "Thanks for your concern. I've reported the theft to the police. Hmmmm. Yes. Everything else is under lock and key. Hmmm. I appreciate the offer, but I have it already taken care of."

The Wyrm reached over and grabbed one of the bats from the basket, pulling it softly from the others. Hank Aaron's signature stood out, black ink against the blonde wood. Behind him, out in the real world, there was another cheer from Wrigley.

"No, no, nothing immediate. They're sending someone over later," the old man gave a laugh, "I hope so. I gave up tickets tonight. Bleacher bums, but still...And I do want to get back to the game."

The Wyrm drew the bat back over his shoulder, extending one foot forward, planting the other behind in a classic stance. Professor Duncan's head was a shiny baseball planted on top of a practice stake.

"Uh-huh," said the old man, impatient now. "Uh-huh. No, I have to go. Tomorrow at school. G'bye." He cradled the phone with one hand, set the baseball down with the other, and reached over to turn up the radio.

That was when he saw the Wyrm. Professor Duncan opened his mouth to shout something, and the Wyrm brought the bat around in a level, clean stroke, right above the shoulders.

The walls resounded with the sharp crack of a broken-bat double. The crowd at Wrigley rose to their feet and bellowed their approval. The Professor half-slid, half-fell out of his chair, the side of his head caved in. He made a weak, gurgling motion, his good eye wide with fear as he looked up at the gargoyle figure of the Wyrm.

The Wyrm raised the shattered stump of the bat with both hands, like a vampire-hunter with a stake. He straddled the professor, who raised one hand weakly, trying to ward off the blow.

The doorbell rang, a sharp electric sound.

Then a knock. Then a muffled female voice, calling the professor's name. Then the unmistakable sound of the doorknob turning. Duncan did not lock his front door. The Wyrm dropped the remains of the bat, and stepped back onto the fire escape.

The front door swung open and the female voice called again, "Professor Duncan!"

Something dropped out at the bottom of Justin's gut. The voice belonged to Lt. Alexandra Stone.

The Wyrm pressed himself against the sooty dark side of the apartment building, the texture of the bricks and mortar pressed against his wings, transposing their rough, random patterns onto his flesh. He could no longer see into the room.

Footsteps came closer. Then a curse as she saw the body of the Professor. Then some fumbling, and the soft beeping of numbers punched into the telephone. Alexandra's voice now, sharp and commanding. "Lieutnant Stone. Emergency." The address was given. Hang-up, a cautious step towards the window, then a second.

The serpent at the base of Justin's brain coiled in exasperation. The Dragon reached out to him. There should be no witnesses, it said. There should be no survivors. He failed to guarantee that earlier. Now he failed again to silence someone with knowledge of the Dragons Beyond.

Justin willed himself still. Don't look out the window, he thought, speaking to Alexandra, not to the Dragon. Don't make yourself a victim.

Then a wet, gurgling noise from the fallen professor, and the footsteps retreated. Alexandra's voice again, this time quiet and indistinct, as she spoke to the wounded man.

Justin leapt off the scaffolding of the fire escape, hurtling twenty feet before he had to spread his wings. He sailed down, into the arms of a large oak.

He settled on one of the great branches, and turned with serpentine grace in the same move. He had rattled the fire escape in his departure, and now Lt. Stone stood at the window, trying to divine the darkness. Her hair was worn free now, and radiated like a halo around her. She

leaned out to look up and down the scaffolding. Then she pulled herself back in.

Sirens were in the distance, growing louder. The Wyrm growled and launched himself from his arboreal perch. He glided noiselessly down the street, just above the lights, and only started to beat his wings when he was halfway down the street from the apartment complex. Cursing, he flapped his way back to his loft above the bookstore, keeping to the darkened parts of the city, crossing the brighter streets only when he had to. It took him a half-hour to return to his lair.

The serpent-voice was quiet in the back of his brain, but it was not a peaceful silence. Justin could feel the gathering storm coming, the wrath of the Dragon.

He dropped through the skylight and Shifted back into human form. The bottom of his stomach, lost on the fire escape, had still not returned.

Come to me, my childe, chuckled the Dragon, speaking from the heart of his mind. *Come to me, my Wyrm.*

With heavy feet, Justin opened the door to the Hall of Mirrors. No candles needed to be lit. The Dragon was there already, his long dark face in every mirror, his eyes glowing with a hellish radiance the reflected off every surface.

The Dragon rumbled. *"The one who brought the Dragonstooth Blade, the Drokpa scholar, he is dead."* The question was put as a statement.

"I left him a dying man," said Justin calmly and truthfully.

"Kneel before your master," snapped the Dragon. Justin dropped slowly to his knees, looking into the mirrors, seeking a clue of his disposition. Nothing there but smokey flesh and blazing eyes. Again, the thing in the mirror asked, *"The one who brought the Dragonstooth Blade, he is dead."*

"I hit him with a blow that would kill five of his kind," said Justin, "I do not think he survived."

"You did not check," rumbled the creature in the mirrors, *"You did not make sure."*

"I was interrupted in my work," said Justin quickly. Inside, he thought. *You know this. You are part of me. Why ask!*

The Dragon sneered. *"You were interrupted. And you did not kill the interruption as well?"*

That was the question. Justin's throat tightened, and his lips grew dry. He stammered. "I recognized the interruption, and...thought that disposing of her would lead to too many questions. Her death would connect the other deaths together."

He held his other thoughts, the thoughts that he did not want to have to kill this Alexandra, as far away from the base of his brain as he could. He was embarrassed by the idea, and embarrassed by the way he had to hide it from his Master.

The dragon in the mirror was silent for a moment. *"Good,"* he said at last, *"There is much to be done in this city, and it would be inconvenient for you to leave at the moment."*

Justin let himself relax, exhale deeply. He had done the right thing.

A sudden spasm gripped Justin like a clawed fist, immobilizing him. Still on his knees, he slammed forward, smashing his face against the hardwood floor. He raised himself up, then slammed himself down again. A third time, and a fourth. By the fifth time the blood was leaking out of the corner of his mouth, his eyes glassy from the pain.

Within, he tried to restrain the Dragon's actions, to keep it from hurting him, but the creature in the mirror was too strong, its grip at the base of his brain too powerful. It was like a firm hand grasped him at the base of the neck and pitched him forward, again and again. Any protests to stop were like butterfly wings struggling in a raven's beak. He did not beg or cry, but took his punishment.

At last, after maybe a dozen buffets, the pounding ceased. Justin saw himself in the large, cheval glass mirror. Red welts rose on both sides of his face, and his forehead was already purple-black from the impacts. His lower lip was split, and he gurgled up thick, heavy blood. Somewhere in the distance, a phone rang.

"Remember, my Wyrm," said the Dragon, *"I take failure badly. I can punish. I can also heal."*

As Justin watched, the bruises and lacerations began to fade, burrowing deep within the skin, out of sight of prying eyes. The split lip began to close up, even the blood began to fade back into the skin.

"Punishment and healing both take energy on my part, Wyrm," hissed the Dragon, angry as a steam kettle, *"So does keeping track of you from a distance. But for you I am willing to pay that cost, best of my servants. I own you body and soul! See to it I don't have to reprimand you again in this matter!"*

With that the Dragon winked out, as sharp and distinctly as a TV set turning off. Justin winced at the feeling of the serpent's presence suddenly cutting off from him. It would be back, but in the time it would be gone, the loneliness would be as intense as any physical damage.

Justin reached up and touched his once-shattered flesh. It was unmarked, but sore. His tongue still tasted the slightest bit of blood from his cut cheeks. Unsteadily, regaining control of his body, he rose and padded back into the main room.

The message machine blinked an incessant crimson. He punched the play button and made a bee-line for the whiskey in the kitchen.

"Justin, it's Alexandra," spat the machine, "Don't ask how I am, the answer is horrible. I need your expert advice again. Can you do dinner tomorrow? Call my machine and tell me if it's OK." She gave a number and rang off.

Justin sat down next to the machine, and played it again, then a third time. The whiskey stung in his mouth. She said she needed advice. Expert advice. Business, probably dealing with the sudden death of Professor Duncan.

Dinner. She said dinner, as well. An off-the-record meeting, or something more?

Justin rose and slowly closed the door to the Hall of Mirrors. He stared at the phone for a while. Then he picked up the receiver and punched in the number Alexandra had left.

VI

🦂 🦂 🦂

ALEXANDRA HAD SUGGESTED mid-eastern and Justin knew a place north of Armitage that served great lamb. It was a hole-in-the wall joint, ten feet across and a full block deep. Pictures of Danny Thomas hung on the walls, and wailing young men played plinking melodies on the CD system.

Justin liked the place, if only because the owner and maitre d' described the daily specials in a manner that would win an acting award. The specials for the day were a boneless chicken breast cooked with a long list of exotic spices, most of which were brought fresh to the restaurant from Lebanon, served on a bed of rice with a side of spinach pie, and lamb chops, lovingly marinated for the last decade in a special wine sauce and served with the aforementioned rice. Both came with salad, and hot pita bread, just pulled from the oven.

Alexandra smiled at the presentation, then ordered the shish kebab. Justin did the same, and ordered a plate of kibbe nayee, a raw lamb appetizer. A bottle of white zinf with the appetizer, and coffee with dinner.

The raw lamb was perfect, served with olive oil and pine nuts, soft enough to be scooped up with the fresh-baked pita bread. Alexandra was a little hesitant at first, but the lamb was tender and literally dissolved in her mouth. She had struck Justin as tense and worried when she picked him up, but the lamb and wine relaxed her some. She made appreciative noises and was soon licking raw lamb from her fingers.

"Not to bring you down," he said, "But how's business!"

"Business sucks," she said flatly, her eyes turning serious over the edge of her wine glass. "The good news is that the entire occult angle has been missed by the media. The Trib reported the fire in the Metro section, section two, page three, as a tragic misadventure — the lesson being don't play with fire and drink. The *Sun-Times* didn't even have that much. Thanks for not going crazy about the media being brought in."

Justin shrugged, "I'm a professional," he said simply, "I don't need the publicity."

"You might not want it, but you might get it. Because this entire thing may have a definite cult angle," said Alexandra.

Justin raised his eyebrows. "Lieutenant, I didn't think you were one to believe in ghosts and demons."

Alexandra smiled, "Professor, you know that it doesn't have to have monsters leaping from the woodwork to have a cult angle." She stopped and frowned over the wine.

The silence lengthened between them, "Sorry," Justin said, "I forgot this was an 'expert advice' session."

"No, it's not that," Alexandra waved an invisible fly away from her face. Another silence. "We lost the survivor. You know. You were there."

Justin paused for a moment, thinking of the boy's body spiraling down to the concrete below. "I'm sorry. I was surprised anyone could have survived that fire in the first place."

"He survived," said Alexandra, "He apparently recovered enough to pull himself out of bed, pull his tubes loose, break open the window with both arms in casts, and jump. Sound likely to you!"

Justin shook his head, slowly. "So what are you doing?"

Alexandra leaned back and sighed, "Me? Nothing. Not my jurisdiction. This is city police. But they brought in the drug boys, one of whom is an old friend."

Justin shot her a questioning look and she quickly, too quickly, added, "We went to the academy together. Cop network. We share things. Anyway, they found non-prescription medication in him. Street stuff, pretty pure and pretty lethal. Weird thing is, the same stuff was found on a dead junkie two blocks away."

"Overdose?"

"Homicide. Someone tried to paint a wall with her brains."

Justin held up the last bit of the pita, kibee dribbling from the end, "And you bridle at raw lamb!"

She snatched the piece of bread from his fingers and popped it into her mouth. "Doesn't it strike you as odd?" she said.

"Odd? A bit," said Justin, "But how many people die every day in Chicago? The problem with most cult investigators is that they see secret societies and cults everywhere. Once you start looking at things like that, everything becomes linked in one big conspiracy."

"You sound like my superiors," snorted the policewoman. The waiter arrived with the salads—big plates of lettuce decked with feta cheese and garnished with olives and radishes, smothered in a thick vinegar dressing. "The barn incident is settled, and the kid leapt in Chicago, which is Cook County's problem. Anyway, we did find out where the kids got the dingus, the funny-looking axe."

Justin shook his head, "I thought we were both too late."

"We were. But the kid was awake in the ambulance, remember. One of the EMTs is a friend of a friend, and told me that he was shouting about demons and angels and was calling for his uncle, until they put him under."

"He got it from his uncle?" said Justin, biting into a slice of radish.

"No uncle, I checked," said Alexandra, "But then my dope squad friend sent me another report. Seems a U of C professor had a break-in at his office. Kids, who made off with an old artifact he brought back from the East. Prof's name was Duncan."

"Ahh," said Justin. "Uncle. Duncan. Your EMTs missed the name."

"Right," she leaned forward over the table. Justin could smell her subtle perfume. "And guess what happened when I visited him!"

"Leaped out a window!" asked Justin with a straight face.

"Close," said Alexandra. "Someone got there just before me, and clobbered him with a baseball bat."

"Good lord," muttered Justin, "Did you see the attacker?"

"Went out the fire escape," said the policewoman. "No other witnesses. The old guy hung on long enough, though, to tell me where to look for information. It was real important for him, vitally important, to show me his collected papers on the Dragon People, your Drokpas. He volunteered to do this without my prompting, and managed to do that with half his head caved in. He gave me a key, too, which I've got someone tracking on. How does that add into the equation?"

"I think I see your point," said Justin, rubbing his chin, "One set of deaths is fate, a second coincidence. After three it just starts looking sloppy. You think there are really rival cults battling in Chicago." He said it as a fact. "Like mystic gangbangers."

"I don't know what to think," said Alexandra, "I'm still reading all the material the old man gave to me. It's a fistful, but it gives a very different read on the history of your dragons."

The main course arrived, two skewers of juicy lamb mixed with potatoes, onions, tomatoes and peppers. Justin used his fork to slide the cubes of meat and vegetables off the spike onto the rice. "Oh? Some different scholarly interpretation of the old legends?"

"Different set of sources, apparently. Remember you telling me about the Dragons being driven out, and the Dragon of the West being set up as the guardian?"

"That's how I learned it," said Justin, sounding mildly hurt.

"And probably from western sources. In the east, where Duncan was doing his research, the story is very different."

Justin shoved a bit of meat into his mouth and waved at her with the empty fork to continue.

"OK. Long ago, before recorded history, dragons ruled men. The men grew restive under the dragon's yoke, and some of the dragons agreed to leave this world for men to rule on their own. In Duncan's notes, these are identified as the Dragons Beyond, the Eastern Dragons. They left voluntarily, it says, but would return for the final battle between good and evil. They left their wisest followers, the Drokpas, or Dragon People, who have a temple in Tibet, near Butan.

"The Dragons of the West remained on Earth, and were hunted down by men over the years. They became sworn enemies of man, and their most powerful member, the Great or True Dragon, was the most evil of the group, and sought nothing less than domination of the world. Finally, with the aid of Drokpa holy men from the East, a group of medieval monks defeated the Great Dragon. They could not kill him, for he was too powerful, but rather banished him to a netherworld halfway between us and wherever the other dragons went to, where he could no longer hurt mankind.

"The Great Dragon is no guardian, according to these sources, but rather a greater danger than the elusive Dragons Beyond, who are only supposed to come back for the end of the world, not to cause it. Supposedly the Great Dragon of the West still seeks to rule mankind, but his first step is to destroy the followers of the Eastern Dragons. Supposedly these Eastern Dragons might return, and that scares the spit out of the Great Dragon of the West."

The lamb was tender, a choice cut, but it tasted bitter in Justin's mouth. Within his mind, the serpent-touch of the Dragon remained silent, but the words still bothered him. Yes, that could be a story put forward by the Drokpas, to cover their actions against his Master. He had heard tales like that before.

"So you think that someone is killing those who have Drokpa contacts!" he said at last. "That there is a cult of this Great, True Dragon!"

"Exactly," said Alexandra, leaning back in

her chair. The maitre d' took this as a sign to ask if everything was all right, and could he offer them something for desert. Justin politely declined, then looked at Alexandra. She popped her last bit of lamb in her mouth and said, "No. I'm on duty in another two hours."

"Night Owl," said Justin.

"I am brother to Dragons, companion to owls," said Alexandra. "Book of Job. I've been checking other dragon references as well."

"That's just one translation of the verse," said Justin, "Another is 'brother to Jackals, companion to Ostriches.' It's supposed to show the man outcast from society. Job is lamenting he is so cursed that even other outcasts will have nothing to do with him."

"Ostriches?" said Alexandra, giggling, "No way."

"Way," said Justin, "Just as there was no apple in the garden of Eden, either. Apples weren't in the Middle East. Translations give you all sorts of trouble, which is one reason there are different versions of the same tale. Now, where does this leave you officially?"

"Like I said, nowhere," said Alexandra "There is no case for me to officially handle. Duncan and the leaper are both out of my neck of the woods. But there's something linking all this together, and it's likely the dingus, the funky blade. I had one of our forensic guys look at it. You know what it was?"

"Fossilized dinosaur tooth," said Justin, "That was my guess before."

"Bone," she said with a smile, "Not stone, but real bone, ancient, preserved for years."

Justin whistled, then shrugged, "No wonder Duncan reported it missing. There are all manner of preserved relics. I told you before that saints and heroes often had their bones preserved in swords and reliquaries."

Alexandra, nodded. "Yeah, but no one knows what species this bone belongs to. A real bone from the age of the dinosaurs is bad enough, but one no one knows about?"

Justin was quiet. "I have no idea what it means."

"Neither do I," said Alexandra, "Do you want to help?"

"Help?"

Alexandra shrugged "This is all on my own, but I need an expert. If you're interested, I have most of Duncan's files."

Justin was quiet for a moment. He sought advice in the depths of his mind, but the Dragon was elsewhere, or was not talking to him. "Yes," he said, "I'd like that very much."

They chose to have desert after all, cheesecake at a small cafe down the street. The rest of the evening was small talk. The weather. A new exhibit down at the Field Museum. Family (she had none, he claimed distant relatives in England). Art (he admitted to drawing a bit, but said it never went anywhere). The current Cubs home stand. At last she dropped him off at the bookstore, en route back to the job.

As she slowed the Cherokee, she laid her hand on his. Justin's heart skipped a beat.

"Thanks," she said.

"For what?" he said, his throat suddenly tightening.

"For saying you'd help. For being here. All this is just a little bit weird. It's good to have someone who knows what is going on."

"Or pretends to," said Justin, unsure what he meant by it.

Alexandra laughed. "Tomorrow night. My place. You free?"

Justin agreed without thinking. Alexandra gave an address, said she would treat for dinner. Then they could go through the information Professor Duncan gave her there. Justin climbed out and Alexandra pulled back out into traffic, waving as she drove off.

Justin stood in the street, watching her red tail lights merge with the others on the highway, then turn westwards after three blocks.

Even after she was gone he stood there, letting the sounds of the area filter through. Somewhere around him a couple was arguing hotly. A child was crying. Someone was singing passionately off-key to a Heartbreakers song. A dog howled at something invisible.

But the Dragon, the Guardian of the Gates, his Master in the Mirror, remained silent in his mind.

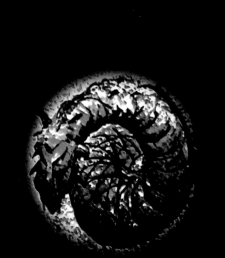

VII

🌿 🌿 🌿

THAT NIGHT, JUSTIN dreamed. His dreams were normally ordinary dreams, dreams which would remain fuzzy and unimportant upon waking, half-remembered vignettes from an alternate life. Sometimes they would leave a black feeling of deep brooding, or a bitter taste in his mouth, but otherwise they were simply dreams.

Tonight, he dreamed a memory.

Half a world away, in England, the Sterling family estate was no more than a ruined, overgrown foundation, the family name dead and gone, its history erased, its heritage lost. Now he walked among those ruins in his dreams, and they slowly returned to life. The stone walls rebuilt

themselves and slathered themselves in plaster, the woodwork restored itself from splintered dust, the wall hangings reknitted themselves. Outside, the weeds and gorse retreated to reveal a manicured lawn beneath, a place for the sheep to gambol and bleat.

Yet the house remained empty. Justin's call brought no answer.

And I was the only one who lived to tell the tale, Justin thought in the dream. He, Sir Justinian, Earl of Sterling, was the only one of this household to escape the plague, the Black Death. And that was by accepting the Dragon as his master.

The Death was one of those regular waves of devastation that swung through the Continent in those days, carried on the backs of rats and in the itching garments of the pedlars. At first he and his fellow lords had thought it was a foreign problem, and they would be safe as Englishmen, secure behind their channel. Then it reached London and it was a city problem, and they were safe in their country houses. And then the impoverished villiens of the nearby town began to suffer from the weeping sores that spread across their flesh, but the Sterlings and the others of their class thought it a problem of the poor. And then at last it was carried to their doorstep, when the fevers, the chills and headaches crawled within their own bodies, and it then became their problem.

First, his children died of the plague, their small forms laid out in half-sized coffins in miniature funerals. Then the servants perished, and none from the afflicted village would come to the house to replace them. Then the local priest and his parishioners hung the black-skulled sign on the front gate and turned his family's manse into a death house. He watched from his study window as the priest's boys hung the sign, and the fat old priest read the Last Rites through the iron bars, his voice muffled by his heavy woolen scarf. And then none would come to the house at all.

Justin remembered thinking at the time that the quarantine was as much to strengthen the priest's power as it was to protect the community from the wrath of a hateful god.

And then Gwen succumbed to the disease. In the dream he stood at the doorway to her room, watching her lay abed, her porcelain skin now a mottled pattern of boils and pustules dappling her flesh. Wet towels, cool and fresh, seemed to hold the fevers at bay, and give her some respite. Her breathing was soft, but strained. Her golden hair, once worn in ringlets, now spread out on the pillows like a mermaid's locks. He stopped combing it for her only when it started pulling away in handfuls. He, when he was Sir Justinian, would talk to her when she was lucid, and read to her when she was not. His texts were the family Bible and the Classics taken from his own library.

Eventually Gwen would fall asleep beneath her cold wraps, and Justinian would make his way down to the study. The past-Justinian passed the present-Justin at the door, but did not see him. The Justinian of the past was similar to his present self in all the particulars, but a little softer, a little more past middle age, a little more worn around the edges, creased at the eyes and corners of the mouth.

And of course, there were the diseased shadows that moved beneath his skin like submerged spiders. This was the network of the disease itself, which was now starting to blossom into puss-filled boils on his arms and legs. The back of his hands were already a mass of blisters, and his own rest was destroyed by wracking fevers. His cheeks were growing hollow and his skin sallow, and Justin could hear the wind rattle in his breath.

Justin watched his past-self retreat to his own study and drink himself senseless, for it was thought at the time that the water itself carried the pox. The home-distilled whiskey was raw, opened before it had aged a full man's age. Yet Justin thought he would not be here for the liquor to reach its full flower, and he was damned if he was going to leave it to anyone else. Particularly the fat priest who walled up houses in order to enforce god's will.

It was there in the darkness of that study, in the darkness of his soul, that the Dragon first visited him. It manifested in the mirror set upon the desk, a glass mirror imported from the Saracen lands of the east. Mirrors were the gate of the True Dragon, his eyes to the living world. It claimed once that it lay beneath every mirror, waiting and watching. It watched him this night.

Previously, Justinian had tried prayer. He had tried promises and science, astrology and alchemy and folk medicine. He had tried curses and diabolism from old books of his grandfather. Any and all powers he believed in refused to visit, refrained from sparing them of the curse. The room was filled with his failures—the holy relics, the drawn pentagrams, and the smashed barrels, emptied of their whiskey.

At last he railed against the forces of an unforgiving god and an uncaring devil, pulling the books from his shelves, throwing them across the room, tearing the drawn curtains from the windows by their hooks. From outside himself, Justin watched his earlier avatar sweep the desk and tables clean, and rip the pages from the family Bible. He flung the spine against the desk's mirror, but the Saracen mirror did not shatter.

Only then did the Dragon speak to him. It spoke from the center of his being, from the core of his mind, though it appeared in the Saracen mirror, which coiled and vibrated with its own life. At first the diseased Justinian thought it merely a hallucination, a fever dream that the madness of the plague had brought to him. But it was no dream, reassured the spirit in the mirror, the dark spirit with the demon-red eyes. The spirit held the key for his salvation. Health. Undying health and immortal life. And all the Dragon required was for Justin to swear to be his servant for that eternal life.

Justin watched the sad creature he had become, rotted from within by the plague, kneel before the mirror. His own ruined visage was not reflected in the glass, but rather it was filled with the black smoke which coalesced into a reptilian master.

There is a part in all mortal minds, said the Dragon, *the part that sees a cliff's edge and urges you to take that final step.* Justin knew that part well. It was a part that wonders if you would pass out before you strike the bottom. A part that wonders how a knife wound feels, that wants to test an unseen, whirling fan-blade with a finger. A part that wonders what it would be like to inhale the water deep beneath the ice. That part now blossomed in Justin's mind, for the other portions of that mind had been torn away, ripped asunder by the plague and the sight of his emaciated, dying wife.

Justinian accepted the Dragon's offer, quickly and gladly. He took that step off the precipice and into the darkness. Any type of life would be better than the living hell he had been thrust into. He grasped his crucifix and swore his fealty to the beast. He opened his heart and his mind to the darkness.

Except it was not dark. It was warm and red and soft and all-encompassing. Justin felt comforted, drawn within the dragon's heat, his soul, if he truly had one, was laid bare to the Dragon's all-encompassing vision. He reached out to the Dragon, and the Dragon accepted him, and remade him in its image.

In the dream Justin watched his first Shifting, that first time when the Dragon burned the plague from his body, along with every shred of mortality. It hurt worse than any pain he had felt, before or since, and the dream-Justin winced at the sight. He screamed from the pain as blood leaked from his mouth and ears, his hands warping into claws. His very soul was bathed in the Dragon's fire, his body twisted to his new Master's designs. He was forged anew, as steel is tempered and hammered in the forge. He was re-created, and the new creation was free of the blot of disease.

"And I shall call you my Wyrm," said the Dragon, his deep, comforting voice becoming stronger in the back of his mind. *"You shall be my servant on this earth, the Dark Herald for my eventual return, the first among my slaves."*

Justinian looked at his hands and they were no longer hands, but claws, attached to muscular, sinewy arms. He looked in the mirror, and the Dragon was not there. The Wyrm was, its reptilian snout and cold grey eyes regarding Justinian back. Another man's mind might have crumbled at the sight, but the Dragon had picked his servant well. Justin felt new life surge through his body as the Black Death was banished from him. The Dragon had done what no priest or scholar had done—beat the devil's curse.

The voice at the base of his brain said, *"The priest, the fat one who left you for dead. He offends my sense of mercy. Show him the error of his ways. Kill him for me. This is my first demand of you."*

It was all it took, for Justin left the plague house, and swooped down on his powerful wings. Those villagers who were abroad that night might have seen a cathedral gargoyle pass over their fields, or shuttered their windows against the devil himself.

Justinian was full of his new power, and Justin went with him. The past-Justinian was the dream-Justin, and flew with him over the dusk-shrouded fields. He remembered roaring as the wind wrapped around him, and he remembered the Dragon laughing in the back of his mind. After so much pain for so long, it was intoxicating to move without the sharp jabs of pain, to breath without daggers jutting into his lungs.

The priest was his first kill. Justinian took no style in it, no grace. He thundered through the old parsonage to reach his goal. He howled as he landed in the graveyard next to the priest's house, kicking over the rough stone markers laid for the early victims of the Death. The priest's door was barred from the inside but fell in two mighty blows, the splinters radiating inwards as the door finally shattered.

The fat old priest reached for his cross, but neither artifact nor hallowed ground would

the memory usually faded, here the Dragon would coil from its serpent nest at the base of his brain and all would be right in Justin's world. But the Dragon was quiet, and instead he heard a voice, which might have been Gwen's, or might have been Alexandra's.

"I am a brother to dragons," said the voice calmly, "And a companion to owls."

That was not in the past, not a part of the memory. The next part was memory again, though a part he did not want to dwell on. The Wyrm flew back on heavy wings, bellowing in the night wind like a banshee. Justin flew with him, shouting for him to not go on, to turn back, to wake up.

But the dream held its power and would not be denied. Justin's dream-form was back in his study when the Wyrm arrived, and Shifted back into his human form. The past-Justinian stumbled, then examined himself in the mirror. Now he resembled his present-self— his body was unbowed by age or disease, his face smooth and healthy, his eyes bright and sword-sharp. He laughed and it was a hearty laugh, a deep, inhuman laugh. Outside him, the present-Justin shouted to stop, to turn away, to leave. Don't go upstairs. Don't do what you did next.

His past-self ignored the warning, but took a candle and vaulted the stairs two at a time. He had found the way to beat the hell-plague. Now he would cure his Gwendolyne as well!

The door to her room rattled on its hinges as he burst it open. Gwen woke confused and tired. Unsure of where she was, why she was abed. The Past-Justinian leaned close to her and he could smell the pestilence that consumed

save him from the Wyrm's rage. Justin grasped him around the throat with one massive paw, lifting him off the ground. The Wyrm laughed as he tore the priest's vitals out, and within him the Dragon laughed as well. Then the Wyrm ripped the priest's home apart, and set ablaze to the place with the burning pages of the priest's own heavy Bible.

The killing of the priest had given him a feeling of warmth that had not been there for some time. A feeling denied him, a feeling of inclusion, a feeling of belonging. And loyalty. Devotion to the one who had spared him, who had given him his power and renewed his life.

Here the dream was supposed to end. Here

her. Her own mortality stank in his nostrils.

Get away from her, shouted the Justin of the present. Get away from her! Don't do it! But in the Dream he could not move, could not break the bonds that held him like a spirit in his own past.

Gwen's mind cleared slowly, and she reached out with a whithered, boiled hand to stroke Justin's smooth cheek. Justin saw his past-self flinch at the touch, as if a dead thing had risen from the tomb to embrace him. His past-self said the things that Justin remembered, that he had been healed, that the plague had spared him.

A miracle, she had said. Not a miracle, he replied, but a bargain. One that he now wanted to share with her.

She withdrew her hand with a start. Bargain! she said, her words slurred by the thickening of her tongue. Have you gained your life to lose your soul to some devil?

Not a devil, but a savior, Justinian said, pulling Gwen from her bed. She was light as a feather, and did not resist. He half-walked, half-dragged his wife to the large silvered glass mirror that hung against one wall.

The present-Justin screamed for his past shade to stop, and tried to flee the room. He could not, for all the universe of this dream was in this one room. There was nowhere to run to, nowhere to hide.

The Justinian of the past called upon the Dragon to show himself, to save his wife as he had been saved. The mirror darkened, and within that darkness appeared the twin crimson beacon of the Dragon's eyes. It said nothing, but regarded Justinian, Earl of Sterling, and his dying wife.

And Gwendolyne screamed. It was a death-rattle of a scream, weakly rising and falling in a hysterical cadence. She cried for Justinian to spare her, for him to banish the demon, to let her die.

Justinian pressed his crucifix into her hand, "No, he means you no harm. Listen to him, in your mind. Listen to him, and join me in serving him. We can live together forever, you and I."

Her fingers, weeping pus from the boils, closed painfully around the crucifix. "No," she hissed, "It is the devil. God protect me and deliver me from these devils."

"You must!" said the past-Justinian, and the dream-Justin felt himself merging with his former self, the anger enclosing everything around him. He was shouting now, gripping her roughly by the arms. Beneath his fingers Justin could feel the pustules rupturing, the ichor within staining her night-dress. She was crying now, the Lord's Prayer burbling up in wet, raspy breaths.

In the mirror, the Dragon said nothing.

In the dream-memory, Justin felt the Shift upon him, the transformation into the Wyrm, sudden and announced. He fought it as his past-self fought his struggling wife. Deep inside his mind, where the Dragon had first spoken to him, he felt rage, anger, and hatred. He had found salvation for them both. How dare she reject him! How dare she reject his gift!

His arms lengthened and roughened to touch leathery hides, his face elongated into the inhuman muzzle. His claws dug deep into the flesh of her arms, and blood now mixed with the sticky fluid of the ruptured boils.

Gwendolyne, his loving wife, the center of his universe, looked at him and screamed, slamming the crucifix ineffectually against his chest. "Damn you!" she cried, "Damn you to eternal suffering!"

And the present-Justin screamed with her.

The Wyrm was nothing but red rage now. He spun his wounded wife towards the mirror, towards the Dragon. He thrust her forward to accept the creature that had saved him. She would thank him for it, later, when her mind cleared. *Take her*, he shouted through rough, inhuman lips, *take her now!*

Gwendolyne's head bounced off the glass, leaving a spider-web of cracks in the surface. The Dragon was unmoved. The Wyrm slammed her against the mirror, again and again. She screamed weakly at first, then merely cried wetly as she left blood stains on the broken glass. Then there was nothing as the life fled from her, as the Wyrm pounded her dead flesh against the mirror, until at last the mirror itself shattered into a myriad rain of shards.

Sir Justinian of Sterling, the Wyrm of the

Great Dragon, staggered back, the blood of his beloved on his hands. He turned from the human wreckage in the room and fled down to his study. The rest of the universe had come back in the dream, and Justin could again separate from his earlier incarnation. He felt weak and drained and heartsick from the sight.

As he fled, the past-Justinian transformed, returned to the soft thing of mortal flesh and bone and tears. He was crying as he reached his study, the tears as hot and wet as the blood on his hands. He reached out to his desk, to smash the Saracen mirror, the mirror with the Dragon's face in it.

"*No,*" said the familiar voice in the mind. The comforting, lulling, loving voice coiled around at the top of his spine. "*She was weak,*" said the Dragon's voice. "*Her mind was twisted by the plague. She was too far gone. I could have cured her, I would have, if only she accepted me.*"

Justinian looked at the blood on his hands and cursed. The warmth within his mind reached out to him, stroking his feelings, reassuring him.

"*You lost control,*" it said, and the Dream-Justin felt the lie in the voice that he had not heard the first time, "*You could not control your Wyrmshifted form. You will be my servant, my minion, my slave. I will teach you and train you, and make you the perfect weapon against our enemies. And we have enemies, my precious pupil. Enemies who would kill you and banish me to the utter void. You will find them and kill them, and I will make you my perfect weapon.*"

Justin felt the walls of Justinian's heart close around the Dragon, taking that hot warmth to him, taking the beast's comfort. He had failed Gwen, but would not fail his new master. He would be that perfect weapon, that great servant. He would defeat his master's enemies and prepare the way for the Dragon's return.

"*Do not mourn her loss,*" said the Dragon, amused, "*For now you have me.*"

Justin heard the Dragon chuckle, and the chuckle became a laugh and the laugh a hysterical, humorless roar. And Justin felt the years peel back through the dream, over six hundred years since then, always the good soldier, always the perfect servant.

All because his wife would not be damned alongside him. And the Dragon laughed.

Justin sat bolt upright, his body bathed in sweat. The covers of his futon were tangled around him, wet sheets plastered against his body. His breath came in gasps, as if something had been smothering him in his sleep.

He kicked off the sweat-stained sheets and paced in the kitchen, to the place over the sink. He poured himself three fingers of whiskey and sat down again. Outside, the first pink was beginning to show of dawn.

He regained his breathing, and thought about the dream. Thought about the truth.

That was the way it had happened. She had died at his hand, she had cursed him and he had killed her for not following him. And he had not thought of it for years, wrapped in a tight feeling of security, of service, of devotion to the Dragon.

He thought of Alexandra's words, the other side of the history, of the Drokpas. It made sense as well. More sense than the truth he had learned from the Dragon, the truth he had believed for all these years.

What if Alexandra was right? What if his master was not a guardian but a prisoner? That he was fighting not for a better world, but to destroy his enemies?

The bottom dropped out of Justin's world. A new chasm yawned beneath his feet, urging him to take the step into the void.

And at the back of his mind there was the call. *Come to the Hall of Mirrors. Talk to me, my precious Wyrm.* The Dragon summoned.

Justin left the drink untouched on the table and padded obediently into the waning darkness of the mirror-hung room. He lowered himself into a cross-legged position, and carefully, almost gingerly, opened his mind to his Master.

"*I'm worried about your little friend, the policewoman,*" said the Dragon in the mirror, "*I'm afraid we may have to remove her.*"

VIII

T HE WORDS SPLASHED like acid in Justin's stomach. He stammered for a moment, wondering how much of the dream the Dragon had known of, and at the same time wondered how much of the dream the Dragon had caused.

"She knows too much," said the Dragon, *"Too much about about us. Too much about what you have done. It is time to remove her, in an accidental fashion."* Its voice was low and relaxed, as if it were discussing putting down the family pet with Fido in the room.

"I don't think she does," said Justin, "And I think removing her will create more problems than it is worth."

The Dragon chuckled. It was not a pleasant chuckle, but one of cracking bones. *"I cannot be everywhere at once, but I can be anywhere. I have looked through the mirrors in her life, and in the lives of those around her. Her actions are on her own, supported by no one besides herself. An untimely death would do no damage to us. No damage to our eventual plans."*

"With respect, Lord," said Justin, stomach churning, "I think that she may be dissuaded from pursuing. It has happened before when an enemy has been deflected without destruction. Or even turned to our advantage."

The Dragon in the mirror was silent. Justin steeled himself for another round of discipline. Instead, calmly, it said, *"Open yourself to me, Wyrm. Open your mind fully to me. Explain why you risk my anger over such a minor matter."*

Justin realized he had been holding his breath, and exhaled slowly and cautiously. He shook his loose hair back out of his eyes

and began to mentally let down the barriers around his mind. To let the Dragon move through his thoughts fully, to escape from the pit of his brain and move unimpeded through his mind.

He let the memory of the past few days spill out easily, effortlessly. He did not attempt to hide his interest in Alexandra, nor her similarity to Gwendolyne.

Yet he did hold one piece tight to him, denying that even to the Dragon's questing probes. The dream, the horrid dream that brought back the memories of the past. The dream that tested his devotion. He was ashamed of the thoughts and scared of them at the same time, and did not want his Master to uncover them, to drag them out into the light.

He could feel the Dragon's energy moving through his mind, its serpentine tendrils snaking through his mind. He imagined one tendril poking at the memories of the dream, but, rebuffed, moved to other sections of his brain.

After a short while, the warm tendrils pulled back, retreated to the bottom of his brain. The Dragon chuckled.

"So, this one has caught your eye," said the Dragon, *"I thought that part of you had been burned out forever. You are my Wyrm, my Servant, my Minion. You belong to no one but me. Yet I will grant you the boon. Turn the woman from her investigations, convince her to investigate other matters. Set her on the wrong course. If you do that, then I will spare her. If you do not, she must be neutralized. You will have to kill her."*

Justin bowed deeply to his master. When he

looked up again, the only face that reflected in the mirror was his own. The face was tightly drawn and worried.

Justin punched the telephone for Alexandra, expecting to get her machine. Instead she was there, her voice worn after the evening's work. The next night was her 'day off,' so they could have a leisurely dinner and then sit up and examine the notes. Justin suggested seafood and Alexandra said she knew just the place, not too far from her apartment.

The place was on the first floor of an office building under the flight path of O'Hare. Jumbo jets grumbled and roared overhead. It was unassuming from the outside, looking no more than a lunchtime bar-stop for harried executives. But beyond the bar was a wide, darkened dining area, the booths separated by lit tanks filled with tropical fish.

The seating was such that they sat side by side, facing outwards. Justin could feel her warmth. She had chosen a black turtleneck, a white half-coat, and white leather skirt that dropped to the knee. The shirt and turtleneck clung to her like a second skin.

"Police work pays this well?" he said, looking at the restaurant's furnishings.

"Special evening," she said, "So I raided my piggy bank."

She had the shrimp scampi. He had the orange roughie. The fish was tender to the point of almost disintegrating on the fork. Chardonnay with dinner, hot tea afterwards. Talk of England and painters, and the Art Institute and the latest scandal in Washington. Eventually, the conversation circled and descended, like a spacecraft caught below a black hole's event horizon, down to Duncan's files, and the True Dragon.

"From the notes, there may be a connection," she said, "That connection being the Dragonstooth blade. It belonged to Duncan, brought back from a dig in Kurdistan. The writing on the tomb wall that was found with it said the artifact was fashioned from the jawbone of one of the Western Dragons, the ones who remained after the Eastern Dragons left. This particular Dragon, identified as Rabbah in the texts, was killed by a Persian hero, using a sword fashioned with the finger-bones of a Drokpa scholar in the hilt."

"Right," said Justin, "I think I mentioned it before, that heroes and saints would often have parts of their bodies instilled into reliquaries, which were purported to have magical abilities."

"Uh-huh," she motioned with her fork, prawn impaled on the tines. "Well, they thought highly of them in this particular one. Duncan's group apparently found the hero's tomb, and it was a jackpot as far as Duncan was concerned. They lifted a pile of black metal plates out of the excavation. That story I told you last night about Eastern and Western Dragons was from the translation of the plates."

"Interesting," said Justin, "Hold on a moment. Is there one Western Dragon or a number of Dragons?"

"At the time of the tomb, a couple hundred centuries BC, there were a couple of dragons. There had been a war between man and the surviving Western Dragons, the ones that had not left. Rabbah had his own master, who is unnamed, only called The Great Dragon."

Was Rabbah another servant of yours, master? thought Justin, but the serpent in his brain made no response.

"Duncan pulled later material from folktales in Hungary, and pretty neatly connected the Great Dragon mentioned in the tomb with the Last True Dragon that the monks had banished in the Middle Ages. Both are described as beings of smoke and darkness, their eyes red from hatred of the living."

"Impressive," said Justin, shifting uncomfortably in his seat. "But keep in mind that histories and legends tend to be written by

the victors. I'm sure the followers of the Great Dragon, the one vanquished by these monks, would tell you a different tale. You don't really believe all this, do you?"

"In itself, no," she said, and Justin felt himself relax a moment. "Its Gilgamesh stuff, Joe Campbell 101, ancient legends from forgotten peoples. How it connects with us is that someone *does* believe it."

"Who?" said Justin, his stomach tightening again, "Duncan was a researcher. Your supposed cultists were college kids. Who believes in this?"

"The killer," said Alexandra simply, and watched Justin lean away from her.

Justin blinked, half expected other policemen to emerge from the darkened booths with handcuffs and night sticks. "Killer?" he managed.

"Imagine someone out there who has access to this material, or a twisted version of this material. Believes in this Great Dragon, and chooses to be his servant. Someone who gets sucked into the entire belief of the Great Dragon, such that he becomes his Holy Avenger. The Great Dragon is his god, and he

is willing to kill for his god."

Justin nodded. "Self-delusion is often a key part of cult behavior. First in the founder, then spreading outwards."

"I think the killer is one man," said Alexandra, "Knowledgeable, probably nondescript. Believes he is the Dragon's Chosen One. Somehow he sees the boys with the Dragonstooth blade, or finds out they are planning a Eastern Dragon ceremony. He attacks them and sets fire to the barn. He trails the survivor and shoves him out a window. Then he tracks the axe back to Professor Duncan and bludgeons him."

"Hold on, now," said Justin. "The boys died of the fire, the surviving lad was a suicide, and Duncan was a random attack."

"That's the way it looks," said Alexandra solemnly, "And if you put me on the stand or in front of bank of cameras, I would agree. But remember the lacerations on the bodies, the ones you thought of as animals. And how did the leaper break open the window with two busted arms! It's only supposed to raise up an inch or so. And where did the drugs in his system come from? Remember the junkie with the smashed head in the alley. And why the attack on Duncan so close to the others!"

Justin rubbed his chin solemnly. "Hmmm. It could be...no, it's likely nothing more than chance occurrences. Serendipity. The lacerations were from splinting beams. The window was already broken. The drugs were already in the boy's system, and the EMTs missed it. The attack on Duncan was a prowler. Taken together, they can be knitted into a conspiracy, but that's the nature of a conspiracy, a collection of evidence which leads to some unprovable goal."

"But if there is a Chosen One…" began Alexandra.

"If there is, he has to have known the boys in advance, and known about their midnight ceremony. That suggests another student or a teacher. He has to have known about the sur-

vivor and been able to get into the youth's room. That suggests a doctor or nurse. He has to have known about the axe and find out where it came from. That might be someone who has access to the police. And he has to have been able take out nine young men at a time. That..." he waved his hands, "suggests something out of a bad sci-fi movie."

"Perhaps you're right," said Alexandra, "Maybe I'm making too much of nothing."

Justin nodded enthusiastically. "A few years back, someone told me that the secret sign of a conspiracy was that it was connected with the number five. And if you looked hard enough, everything is connected with the number five. Understand!"

Alexandra laughed, a small, warm laugh.

"There is always a conspiracy, if you look hard enough."

"And if there really is such a servant of the Great, True Dragon," added Justin, putting his hand on hers, "I really don't want him coming after you."

Alexandra laughed again, "Right. It's so much safer fighting the druggies and killers and rapists out there." But she did not move her hand away from his.

The conversation moved on to other matters. The gang on the night shift at the station. Life in Wicker Park with the young art students. Commuting. Basketball. Life.

As the evening progressed, he felt the Dragon's tug at the base of his brain. Just a presence, an awareness, a potency that resided within him, his link to his Master.

They got into her Jeep, "I've got Duncan's notes at my place," she said, "Want to come up and take a look!"

Justin shrugged and smiled, "Come up and see your etchings!"

"Something like that."

"I suppose," said Justin.

Her place was a few miles west, in a pile of factory-assembled condos. The buildings were clones of each other, differing only by location and the number of slender saplings planted in the brown earth of the unsodded lawn. The development was at the end of a cul-de-sac. Two other similar condo units, unfinished, stood guard nearby, skeletons of pale wood.

Justin felt the Dragon was back, coiled at the base of his brain, watching and waiting.

"The place is popular with airline pilots,"

the landing. Her door keys were in hand.

"Missed a step," said Justin, and tried to forcibly shove the Dragon back into the base of his mind. The Dragon grumbled and threatened, but slowly retreated.

Her apartment was furnished in first-time-renter's style. A low coffee table. Matching sofa and chairs from a company specializing in making everything of two-by-fours. An entertainment center with both a CD player and turntable, the old vinyl albums stashed beneath. Kitchen nook with only one pan, clean, on the stove. A short hallway led back to the bathroom and bedroom. A framed poster of Chicago hung on the wall, a mirror in a pressed-wood frame stood guard by the door. The apartment had not been occupied long.

The coffee table was ladened with papers and notebooks. Many of them were curling photocopies of rubbings, likely taken from the tombs of the Persian hero. A small cardboard box held a stack of rough, lozenge-shaped metal plates.

said Alexandra, rummaging for the front door key, "Which means either there's loud parties, or I get the place to myself."

Justin hesitated, "Maybe I should go," he said, "It is kind of late, and whatever is in Duncan's notes I can get later."

Alexandra leaned forward, into his arms, and pressed her lips against his. They were soft and tasted of human tears.

"Come on," she said, and led him up the stairs to his apartment.

She must die, said the Dragon, simply and quietly, deep within Justin's brain.

She's going to drop the investigation, said Justin silently to himself. *You heard that.*

She must DIE! said the Dragon, and pulled the mental leash tight. A pang of pain lanced through the back of Justin's mind. He stumbled from the suddenness of the blow.

"You OK!" said Alexandra, from the top of

And laying across the top of the box was a sword. It was a long, heavy weapon, narrow in the body and widening slightly at the tip. It glimmered in the light of the overhead fixture. The hilt was long and seemed to have a long golden crystal set into the wrappings.

"Make yourself comfortable," said Alexandra, "I've got to get out of this dress. Too much to eat, I'm afraid." She paused to hit the play button on the stereo. A Motown beat, turned down low, issued from the speakers.

Justin lowered himself onto the sofa, and picked up the sword. It had an electric feel to it, as if it was charged with its own power. It felt dangerous, a danger that chilled him to the bone. The long crystal was a yellowing amber. Within it was small whitish column. A human finger bone, set in the gem.

What is it? snarled the Dragon.

A sword, he thought back.

Show it to me, said the Dragon.

It's a sword, he repeated.

SHOW IT TO ME! snarled the Dragon in his mind, with another tug. *In the mirror.*

Justin walked to the mirror. Aloud, he said, "Where did you get the sword?"

Alexandra shouted from the back room, "Locker. Got the key from Prof. Duncan after the attack, remember! The plates and rubbings were in there, too. He put them in there after the kids stole the dingus from him."

Justin held the sword up to the mirror, and felt a fire ignite at the base of his brain. He winced. The mirror darkened, and cleared to show the face of the Dragon. Its eyes were crimson and wide.

She has the sword! said the Dragon. *She has the Deadly Sword! Its blessed steel can cut you, kill you! Kill her now, before she realizes its power!*

Justin stared at the face in the mirror, the face not his own.

"The Professor's in stable condition, by the way," said Alexandra from the other room, "After the attack I got the key from him, but if he had died, it would have to have been in the evidence locker."

Kill her! said the Dragon in the mirror. *She is a Danger to us! A tool of the Dragons Beyond! Kill her now!*

Justin felt the heat rise within him, the heat of the Shifting. He resisted the growing warmth that spread from the base of his brain, sending tendrils down his spine and through the rest of his body.

No! Justin thought hard, *Don't do this! I can solve this without killing her!*

The fire grew hotter within him, and with it the pain. Centered in his belly, it felt like someone had thrust a hot poker into the center of his being. He dropped to his knees, clutching his stomach.

"No!" he hissed, pleaded, "Don't do this!"

"Did you hear?" said Alexandra, reappearing in the hallway, brushing out her hair. She was dressed in slacks now, and white blouse, buttoned down the front. "Duncan's still in a coma, but at least he's..." Her voice died in her throat.

Justin looked up at her. His eyes glowed like red fire. His face was elongating and his skin was turning leathery and hard. The Wyrm was there.

And trapped within the Wyrm, Justin screamed.

IX

🦎 🦎 🦎

Justin could feel his body transform around him. His limbs became longer, their skin covered with leathery pustules reminiscent of the plague. His face grew heavier as the fang-filled muzzle protruded beneath his eyes. His shirt ripped from the bat-like wings seeking release, his trousers and shoes similarly tearing from the sinewy muscles erupting beneath.

But this time he was not in control. He was not the one welcoming the change. The power of the Dragon, the might of the Wyrm flowed into his body, but did not answer to his will. He tried to stop the Shifting, but it would not stop. He tried to flee, but his misshapened body would not respond.

Within, he flailed about mentally. The Shifting was slowed from his resistance, but still unstoppable.

He tried to shout a warning. All that came out of his mouth was an inarticulate howl.

Alexandra's eyes widened, but she did not wait for the transformation to complete itself. She disappeared into the back of the apartment. When she reappeared she had a portable phone in one hand, a gun in the other.

Of course she has a gun, thought Justin, *she's a police officer.* He fought his body as it tried to rise from the floor. All he succeeded in doing was reducing it to a sluggish crawl.

Lt. Alexandra Stone aimed the gun with one hand, punched buttons with her thumb with the other. Three numbers. Her eyes never left the Wyrm as she dialed.

"Emergency, I have an intruder. 234 Copper Bloom Terrace, Apartment..." Then she screamed as the phone exploded in her hand in a collection of hot shards.

The Wyrm's eyes glowed bright red. Justin struggled against that as well, and they banked, but only slightly. He felt he was trying to restrain the Dragon by physical force. And the Dragon was winning.

It's only harder on you if you fight, said the Dragon to Justin.

"Don't move," said Alexandra, her cheek cut by shattered plastic "Or I will shoot."

The Wyrm laughed and took a step forward, Justin screaming from within. Alexandra's service revolver sounded like a cannon against the bare walls of the apartment. The gun thundered once, twice, and a third time. Red splotches appeared on the Wyrm's hide, then healed over immediately. The Wyrm laughed again.

Justin abandoned restraining the rest of his transformed body, and concentrated on only one limb. Summoning his force of will together, he tried to make the Wyrm kick. One kick, one involuntary twitch of the muscles.

Within him, the Wyrm was thrown off-balance by Justin's sudden lack of resistance, the crumbling of his will. It stumbled for a moment, and in that moment Justin forced the leg to lash out.

The splayed foot caught the sword, the relic-bearing sword that Duncan had brought from the tomb in Kurdistan. The blade danced across the deep-pile carpeting, hilt first. The touch of the blade felt like heated metal against the Wyrm's foot.

Alexandra dropped quickly and came up with the sword in one hand. It was heavy in the blade, and she raised it only waist-high. "What are you!" she said. There was fear in her voice.

"The Dark Herald," hissed the beast, "The Good Soldier of the Great Dragon. I am Death, and I have come for you."

The Wyrm lurched across the room. Within, Justin tried to resist it, but it was like a kitten grabbing onto the foot of a man. Alexandra fired two more shots, then dropped the gun when the beast was three feet away. She grasped the sword with both hands and swung at him, hard.

The Wyrm lurched backwards, but the blade's tip slashed along his chest, from one shoulder to beneath the ribs on the other side. Not a deep wound, but it stung like fire, as if salt had been mixed into the cut.

The Wyrm howled and dropped to one knee. Unlike the bullet wounds, the edges of the cut only knit together slowly and reluctantly. The relic-blade still retained its power.

Alexandra did not wait for the Wyrm to recover, but made a dash past him, for the door. The Wyrm lashed out, and back-handed her into the hallway. Its eyes were blazing with hatred now.

The policewoman kept a firm grip on the sword and fled into the back bedroom. Justin heard the sound of glass breaking and realized that she was trying to get out the window.

The Wyrm pounced, leaping down the hallway to reach the bedroom. She was halfway out the window, sword still in hand, when he reached the room.

The Wyrm grabbed her by the ankle and flung her back into the apartment. She screamed as the broken glass of the window's frame lacerated her thighs and back. Justin smelled the sweet scent of fresh blood. Alexandra flew back across the room, into the mirrored doors of the closet. The doors were knocked from their runners, cheap glass cracking under the force of the blow.

She clung to the sword, and now held it before her, like a protective talisman. Within the Wyrm, Justin could feel the electricity radiating from it. It had tasted dragon blood and lusted for more.

The Wyrm lunged to the left, then the right, but the policewoman kept the tip of the blade between her and the Dragon's servant. She gave one nick on the arm, another small cut on the Wyrm's leathery thigh. Each time the blade cut through his skin like butter, and the wound stung and closed slowly. The room was now wet with both the Wyrm's blood and that of Alexandra Stone.

Alexandra looked tired, her blouse and slacks marred with vibrant splotches of dark blood. The Wyrm was tireless. Within the Wyrm's body Justin felt the pain of the wounds, and a greater pain, seeing the damage his incarnation had inflicted, damage he was powerless to stop. He tried to stop the beast, but all he could hear within was the Dragon's chuckle.

Alexandra took a weary step towards the door, the blade's tip around knee level. The Wyrm interposed himself and lashed out.

She was ready for him, and brought the blade up sharply, into the beast's stomach. Then she pushed hard, using the sword as a spear.

Justin felt the fiery pain lance through him, his entire being bisected by the force of the sword. He could feel the tip of the relic-blade burst from his back, spraying the room with his own foul-smelling blood. Instead of lashing out, the Wyrm curled inward, its taloned arms locked around the blade, trying to pull it out. Alexandra would not release her grip. Justin felt as his entire body would burst into flames at any moment.

And Justin welcomed that.

The Wyrm twisted on the impaling blade, and in Justin's voice said, "I'm sorry, Alexandra. I'm so very sorry."

Within the dying beast, Justin screamed.

Alexandra hesitated, and in the hesitation was lost. The Wyrm twisted, pulling the hilt from her hands. Then it pulled the blade from its belly, withdrawing it from its living sheath.

Alexandra leapt for the bedroom door but the Wyrm was still too fast. It caught her with one taloned claw in the belly and ripped upwards as it struck. The sound of blood-stained fabric and human flesh tearing filled the room, and bright, fresh blood spattered on the walls. With the other claw the Wyrm skewered her through the chest, hard. The wallboard buckled as she slammed into it.

Justin screamed within himself, and in the scream found strength. It seemed to surround him and empower him, drawing from the pain in his own body, from the bloody damage to Alexandra. He saw Alexandra's face, and Gwendolyne's. He saw Professor Duncan, the moustached youth, the junkie, the kids in the barn. He saw the faces of all that he had killed in his long and glorious service to the Dragon.

And he saw the hollowness of that service. The bloody-handed pig-ignorance of it. The trail of bodies and broken lives. And his broken immortal life most of all.

And it made him angry. A new fire burst within his mind, a blue flame of personal anger. The darkness around him peeled back

under the blue fire, and the redness of the Dragon's control hesitated, then fell back under its onslaught.

The Wyrm screamed, shutting its eyes from the pain as within its mind Justin pursued the Dragon. The dark redness fled from his mind, from his limbs, from his body, pulling back at last to the base of his brain, to that secret place where it lurked, waiting for Justin's summons, waiting for the True Dragon's orders.

In his mind, Justin plunged into that redness and grasped the image of the Dragon there behind the head. The Dragon spat poison and fire at him, and Justin mentally squeezed, tightening around the neck of the Dragon's proxy. The beast at the base of his mind coiled under his grip, and spat blood at him. Justin threw that part of the Dragon into the chasm at the base of his mind, and sealed the chasm shut in a blast of azure flame.

And when he opened his eyes again, he was Justin, not the Wyrm. His body responded to him once more.

He was human again, naked from the battle, with heavy red weals where the relic-laden sword had cut him. One ran from one shoulder to under his ribs, another a great, weeping bruise square in the belly, with numerous smaller marks along the arms and legs, as if he had been flogged. The pain rung from every part of his body.

But the body was his. It was his alone.

There was a moan and Justin looked up. Alexandra was folded against the far wall, her body a blasted and broken mass, her arms and legs resting at odd angles. Blood oozed from the corner of her mouth. Her eyes were open and alert, and she impaled him with those blue eyes as she had earlier lanced the beast with her sword. She moaned again.

Justin crawled over to her across the broken bedroom, his strength slowly returning. He cradled her in his arms, but knew there was nothing to be done. The Wyrm had done its work too well.

Hot tears beaded at the corners of his eyes, and began to streak down his cheeks.

"No tears," said Alexandra simply, her voice week and burbling from a punctured lung, "I forgive you. Just get the sunovabitch who did this." Then her eyes grew glassy and her breathing stopped in a long, painful rattle.

Justin laid her carefully on the floor, and sat there for a moment as her flesh cooled and grew stiff. Then he went into the main room. He found a duffel bag and loaded the sword, the metal plates, and papers into it. The sword was cool to his touch.

He pulled from the closet a baggy sweatshirt and sweat pants which fit well enough, and patched together the torn remains of his Doc Martens with duct tape. It would serve for the moment.

The sounds of the sirens were in the distance when he jumped out of the window, and sprawled on the unsodded ground. His boots left deep impressions in the dark earth as he headed back home.

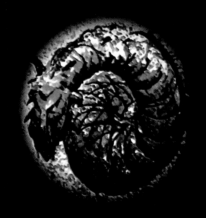

X

✠ ✠ ✠

THE TRIP BACK to his own apartment was uneventful. A short walk across the new construction to the road, a bus to the Metra line, and the rail-car back to Wicker Park. At several times during the trip, Justin felt the familiar flicker in the back of his brain, the warm touch of the Dragon's presence. Each time he burned the feeling out with blue mental fire.

It took over an hour to get home.

The Dragon only spoke to him when he returned to the loft, when he came within the area of the circle of mirrors.

"Come back," it said, *"Open yourself up to me again. Open yourself to my power."*

Justin said nothing. He stripped off the sweats and changed into jeans and a heavy shirt. He looked at the duct-taped work shoes and tossed them in the trash, pulling a set of worn, weathered cowboy boots from a trunk. He began packing the duffel bag with clothing.

"You have to go back there," said the Dragon, *"There are too many loose ends. Even now the police are finding your fingerprints, bits of your flesh. You have to go back. Set fire to the place. Burn it to the ground. You have to go back."*

Justin continued to pack. He pulled the relic-blade out and laid it on the wooden spool table. He left the notes and the box of metal plates within.

"You will obey me!" the Dragon's voice rose in intensity, *"I gave you the gift and I can remove it just as easily! I can bring back the Black Death upon you! I can bring you to heel!"*

Justin felt a sharp pain at the base of his brain, the blossoming of a small headache. He concentrated for a moment, and the pain subsided, wrapped in a cold blue feeling of peace. He continued to pack. He looked around, at the futon, the trunks, the drawing table with its scattered pages, the milk-crate furniture. There was nothing else here he needed.

"Come back and we'll talk," said the Dragon's voice, distant and tinny in his ears, *"Come to the Hall. Let me see you. Let me explain."*

Justin went to the small room bedecked with mirrors. He took the sword with him.

He did not light the candle, but the dragon appeared in the mirrors. In all the mirrors, his smoky face and campfire eyes glimmered.

Justin did not kneel this time.

"I know this was difficult for you," said the Dragon, his voice turning sweet and cloying. *"I know how much she meant to you. But she was a danger. She was too strong. She would never be dissuaded or turned. She would have told others. She was a danger."*

Justin smashed one of the mirrors, the tall dressing mirror, with the sword. Sparks jumped as the blade cut through the glass, and the black smokiness evaporated, leaving only a spider's web of cracks.

"That wasn't nice," said the Dragon. *"I understand you're upset, but you just have to understand. I've always been right before."*

Justin swung at another mirror, the cheval glass one. It blew apart in a maze of small lightning bolts and cascaded to the ground.

"You have no right to do this, Wyrm!" said the Dragon, *"You have no right to fight me! I*

gave you your life! And this is how you repay your debt?"

Another blow, cutting loose a string of rearview mirrors from their mountings. They smashed to pieces as they strung the ground, the reddish light within extinguished.

Justin felt something stir within him, the beginning of a Shift. He thought of Alexandra and the others, and thought of the blue fire of his hatred of the Dragon. The stirring stopped. He remained unchanged. He raised his hand and three more mirrors died.

"At least talk to me," said the Dragon, his voice taking on a plaintive tone, *"You are my best, my favorite servant. I'm sorry if you feel hurt about this."*

Another long blow, dragging against a wall of mirrors. Each mirror burst in turn as the tip of the blade etched its surface. Small bits flew everywhere, but left Justin unmarred.

The Dragon dropped his voice, *"Don't do anything rash. Just think about this for a while. I made you immortal. Undying. What good would she have been in forty years, eighty years? They are simple creatures. They must be protected from the truth out there. We must protect them."*

A convex mirror exploded at the touch of the blade, along with the long dressing mirror. The center of Justin's mind was cold and calm. No dragon fire burned there.

"I'll always be here, you know," said the Dragon, *"I'll be hiding behind every mirror. I'll be waiting. You need time to think. Eventually you'll calm down and we can have a nice talk. You will, you know. You can't hide forever."*

Justin smashed another dozen mirrors effortlessly, silently. Metal and glass cascaded around him.

The only mirror left was the old desk mirror, the one from the land of the Saracens. Most of its silver backing was lost,

its beveled edges chipped by numerous moves. The Dragon was within that mirror, its eyes pleading.

Its eyes filled with fear.

"At least say something to me!" pleaded the Dragon.

"Go to hell," said Justin, and smashed the final mirror.

He stood for a long time in the shattered glass of the room. Slowly he became aware of the sounds outside. The shouts of delivery people, the honking of horns, the shouts of children.

Somewhere, a music student was practicing scales on a clarinet. The sounds were squawky and off-key.

Justin wrote out a check for two months rent, and tacked it to his landlord's door. At the bottom of the check he scribbled, "Sorry about the mess."

He hefted the duffel and walked the two blocks to the L. O'Hare, and where from there!

Butan. Alexandra said the notes pointed towards Butan, in Tibet. There would be the Drokpas, the followers of the Dragons Beyond. The Dragons wise enough to get out, and stay out, and leave man to himself.

Whistling the scales along with the unseen clarinet, Justin Sterling headed east.

EPILOGUE

I N THE WEEKS and months which followed Alexandra's death,
Justinian made his way slowly towards the sanctuary of the
Drokpas in Tibet. If it really existed, if it was more than a whispered legend, he would find it. And within its walls, he would find
the truth, and perhaps, salvation.

He hitchhiked his way to the west coast, found work on a merchant freighter bound for Singapore, and set sail for the Far East. He
took great pains to avoid mirrors and their siren call, but occasionally
he would catch a glimpse of a smoky form and burning eyes in a
polished surface, and turn away, sweating. Occasionally, he would
feel stirrings at the base of his brain, but he would concentrate, call
forth the blue flames of his rage and would soon find peace.

Months at sea gave him time to reflect upon his centuries of existence and the evil which he had done. His heart ached from memories of faces twisted in horror at the sight of the Wyrm, crying out as
its claws tore away their flesh. Men and women, poets and priests
— and never once did he question. Instead, he reveled in his power
and confident arrogance, convinced that he could do no wrong. His
innate sense of good and evil had been completely buried beneath
the great weight of his Master's lies.

No more.

He was finished with it. It was time to make amends for the centuries of murder and destruction, if he could. He would find the
Drokpas, learn their ways and the truth about the Dragons Beyond,
and then, armed with that knowledge, he would take his revenge
on the Dragon.

If there was to be war between them, and there was, he intended
to be the victor. It was his only hope for redemption. His only hope
for peace.

For Gwen. For Alex.

For them all.

THE LORE & SYMBOLS OF

A nciently, there were dragons. They were not creatures of myth. They were creatures of vast power—terrifying to some, threatening to some, godlike and inspiring to others.

Eastern and Western civilizations dealt with the dragons differently. Eastern civilizations revered these wondrous creatures and dedicated priests to their service. As mankind became the dominant force in eastern lands, the dragons feared that their immense power would make mankind too dependent on them, to the detriment of man's own progress. They departed this Mortal realm, but left behind a religious sect dedicated to their service.

Near Butan in Tibet is a temple where live the Drokpas, Dragon People. They have the ability to summon dragons, but they will do so only during the time of Apocalypse, when the ultimate battle between good and evil is fought. That time, they believe, is fast approaching.

Dragons of Western culture had a much more difficult time. They were not revered. They were persecuted and reviled. Considered embodiments of evil, the dragons were hunted down by knights and destroyed. Although they had not been evil, up to that time, the dragons of Western lands soon developed such a hatred for mankind that their true nature was perverted and they lived only for vengeance on their sworn enemy—man.

Eventually, during the Dark Ages, a group of priests succeeded in forcing the last, the greatest and most powerful of these dragons into leaving the mortal realm. The priests could not kill it, but they managed to banish it, imprisoning the Dragon within the Nether Realm.

But though they had imprisoned the Dragon, the priests could not completely cut off its power. Trapped in the Nether World, the Dragon sought

TYRC

WAISE

LERUS

ROGA

EEDER

FIER

PEEI

T'SAN

NGAR

UUR

SEEH

EZIN

THE ANCIENT DROKPAS

 D'GON

 BARSU

 LLAGA

 NHUYU

 AZZAS

 KAI-TE

 CAAI

 MYRRH

 HOPU

 URGAD

 CAHLI

BHULÉ

an outlet back into this world and soon discovered it—mirrors. The Dragon could see through the back of mirrors and into the world from which it had been driven. It began to watch and soon discovered that it could speak to those on the other side of the mirrors, to those looking into the mirror at their own reflections.

The Dragon found that it could speak to some of these men and women and that they would listen and, in exchange for immortal life and eternal youth, they would become the Dragon's Disciples. They pledge their service to one end—the triumph of evil, the return of the Dragon into this world.

The Disciples have no idea that their own destruction must inevitably follow, for the Dragon despises those who serve it.

The Drokpas are an ancient and sacred sect, dedicated to the worship of the Dragons Beyond and mortal enemies of the Great Dragon of the West and his Disciples. Their ceremonies, rituals and symbols are closely-guarded secrets, known only to those initiates who actually dwell and study at the Drokpa Temple in Tibet.

Each symbol represents either one of the Dragons Beyond or a High Priest of the Drokpas. A very few represent great warriors who died in the service of the Drokpas against the Disciples of the Great Dragon. These symbols have been carved from great blocks of marble and line the walls of the Temple's Hall of Elders.

These symbols are also used in sacred texts to identify their wisest and most revered leaders. This also prevents outsiders from knowing the true names of the Dragons Beyond or their followers. For there are Disciples who are schooled in sorcery, and true names are potent weapons which could be used against Dragons Beyond or their priests.

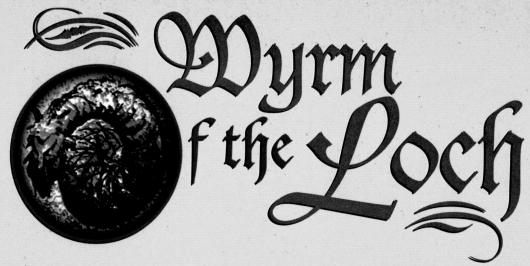

Wyrm Of the Loch

"You will go to Loch Ness."
The face in the mirror was his own—the face of Sir Justinian, Earl of Sterling—but the voice was not his. The voice was a deep, immemorial growl, the sound of something ancient and inhuman.

"You will go to Loch Ness," it repeated. The tones shook the silvered glass in its gold-gilded frame.

Justinian stared into the reflection of his own eyes. They were large and gray beneath his long, white hair. His whole face looked dark these years, haunted since the death of his beloved Gwendolyne. "Loch Ness is in the land of the Scots. Barbarians. What do I care about Loch Ness!"

The voice returned. It grated profoundly, as if the very stones of Sterling Manor were shifting upon each other. *"Your cares do not matter. If they did, your wife would have chosen servitude over death—chosen as you have. Men may call you Lord, but to me, you are less than an errand boy. Do not forget that."*

Justinian had not forgotten, nor could he. As miserable and bitter as his life had been since Gwendolyne's death, it was still life. The Black Plague had taken his wife and the comrades of his youth, but it had not taken him. No, he belonged to the Dragon, who had returned his life on loan, so long as Justinian served.

"How may I serve?"

"You will go to Loch Ness, to the Cameron Abbey. There is a priest visiting there, treasurer of the Church at Glasgow—Robert de Moffethe. Slay him."

Justinian blinked. His first kill had been a priest, nearly fifty years ago, just after Gwendolyne died. Slaying so-called men of God always brought back the piquant grief of his loss. "Another priest? Why!"

"Because it suits me," came the reply.

The Earl of Sterling sighed deeply. He opened his mind to the Dragon. "I will."

Already, the Shifting began.

Justinian's palate stretched forward; teeth crackled and sharpened; nose broadened into a scaly snout; eyes widened and flared vermillion; pupils narrowed to thin black slits; brow sloped back to form a spiky sagittal crest; hair thickened into a prickly mane; ears lengthened to prong points.

He disrobed. Surcoat and waistcoat, ruffles and chemise fell aside as his neck bulged and rippled with scales. Wings budded and sprouted from shoul-

by J. Robert King

der blades, tearing their way outward. Bones achingly lengthened. Chest broadened. Muscles realigned. Skin grew wave upon wave of scales. Hands hardened to talons, nails to claws.

Feeling a strange mixture of disgust and admiration, Justinian watched himself transform. Where once had stood the thin, pale, stately form of a mortal man, there now stood the bulky sinew of an immortal beast. The Wyrm.

"I go to Loch Ness," he hissed. His voice had become a gravelly echo of his master's. "I will slay Robert de Moffethe."

There came a snicker of approval from within the mirror. In the darkness behind the silver, serpentine scales coiled.

"*Seek him beneath the Sacred Stone of Cameron.*" The voice paused, as if expecting to be goaded for more information. When the transformed Earl of Sterling said nothing, the Dragon offered, "*If you must know why you slay him, it is because he has discovered a powerful, ancient artifact of mine—the Mirror of the Loch.*"

"I go to Loch Ness."

✠ ✠ ✠

The highlands, though infested with rag-kilted Scots and blood-feuding clans, were beautiful. Craggy, forbidding, wild, ferocious in the death-pale moonlight. It was the sort of landscape to whet a Wyrm's hunger.

Justinian crouched gargoyle-like atop a rocky massif. His eyes flicked from point to point along the mountain ridges. Just beyond those crags lay Loch Ness. Through splintered clefts, he glimpsed black shards of the lake. Along the line where water met land, there would be a jewel-box of light. Cameron Abbey.

In the abbey was a certain priest who needed to die.

Before all that, though, Justinian wanted food. It had been a long journey to these cold climes—days in caves, nights beneath the moon. He was ravenous. Killing on an empty stomach was a bad idea. Hungry Wyrms were likely to rush things, make mistakes and end up skewered by some errant knight.

There, that fire beside the shepherd's cairn—there will be food in plenty for a hungry serpent.

Justinian launched himself from the granite outcropping. His wings embraced the chill night, the touch of dark to dark. He glided down, talons skimming ragged heather and trickling peat.

Won't the shepherd lad be surprised when Earl Justinian comes to claim a lamb as tribute!

It would be a lad, yes. A man would not waste wood or peat on a fire tonight. There was no fog, no sheeting rain or sleet. The night was only cold, not deadly. It would be a lad, a Scots lad with plenty of freckled bravado and nothing more.

He'll have a tale to tell after this night.

Justinian reached the nadir of his dive. Above, the ragged heights loomed up to swallow the moon. Good. In the black umbra of the hill, he would rise up the belly of night and come on shepherd and sheep unawares.

These Scots were so predictable—flighty and bold and docile by turns, like the longhorn cattle they raised and reived. Cattle.

"Fence them and geld them and herd them and stay clear of their horns," his great uncle, ruler at Sterling Castle in the Midland Valley, had advised. "Most of all, though, make sure the mallet with the first blow. That's how to rule the Scots." Good advice.

Now, to kill with the first blow . . . A final surge of midnight wings flung Justinian up the sheer wall of granite. The moon met him at the pinnacle, above the grassy peak.

Below lay sheep in a thick and murmurous cluster. They huddled close together beneath the frigid moon, as thick as a snowpack. In their midst was a small fire and a stone shepherd's hut. Snoring came from within.

Justinian dropped among the sheep. Claws sunk through tangles of wool and into hot muscle beneath. He pounded down hard atop one beast and heard the wet clack of bones. The grazer never had time to bleat. It lay dead beneath him, a sack of pulverized bone and meat—

What do those Scottish ticks call it—haggis!

He tore a breach in the thing's side and ate. Sweetmeats first—fat and flavor for the laird and sinew and stew bones for the serfs!

Nearby sheep leapt clear, but those farther out still slept. The kill had been quiet, and the feasting was, too.

A collie dashed in among them and began barking. That sent them scrambling away. The dog remained. Its frightened moans were pathetic— the whimpers of an impotent defender as its charge is destroyed.

The collie will awaken the shepherd boy. I do so enjoy dinner conversation.

From the dark doorway came a fierce voice, almost as angry as it was frightened. The boy spoke in Scots' Gaelic—a language that had gone out of style once English showed how to speak without spitting.

Justinian lifted his muzzle. "You'll have to speak English, lad. I'm no Grendel."

"I know who ye are," the boy said. His stern face floated gray and small in the black doorway. "Ye're the Wyrm of the Loch."

Justinian sat back on his haunches and considered. Moonlight cascaded coldly down gory scales. "I suppose I am."

"Ye canna scare me, Anglish Dragon," the boy said. "I've got a cross of Michael, and ye canna take me wi'out his say."

"I canna!" mocked Justinian. "Perhaps I can, but do not want to. Your kind makes for stringy and sour suppers."

"Ye canna touch me. Sarah Cameron says ye took the MacIntosh boys before her eyes, but dinna take her on account of Saint Iona."

"Did she!" said Justinian, pausing to swallow a morsel. "Would this Sarah be from Clan Cameron of Cameron Abbey?"

That question seemed to embolden the boy. He emerged from the shadows and stood uneasily by the cairn. His kilt was filthy and tattered. His hair was a red pelt as matted as the wool of his sheep.

"Ye fear them. That's what Sarah said. That's what her father said, and her grand uncle, the abbot. Ye fear anyone wi' the cross of Michael and guarded by the wings of God."

"A truly fearsome combination, lad," agreed Justinian.

"Ye canna touch us, so ye send yer pagan boys running the hillsides, calling themselves the warriors of the Dragon. But not the Camerons, nor the MacDonnells—not MacDonnell." With that, trembling a little, he held out the dagger he'd drawn from one ragged stocking. "I want none of yer devil gold."

Amusement flickered in Justinian's slitted eyes. "I can tear apart your herd. I can set fire to your huts. I can ruin the proud MacDonnells without ever touching you. Then let's see if you want my devil gold."

"Do yer worst," sneered the boy, though his quivering lip belied the words.

Justinian rose from the gory dinner. "I have already done my worst to your family, Ian MacDonnell. I've taken a sheep and scared the shepherd. In return, you've provided me a hot meal and pleasant conversation. A traveler can ask no more."

Ian swallowed audibly.

"I say good luck to Sarah and her prayers. No cross will save her if the Dragon truly wants her."

With that, Justinian spread wide his wings and

surged into the air. Lamb's blood sprayed away beneath him. The sudden gust seemed to fling the boy back into his cairn, for he was gone from the hilltop. A fourth and fifth beat of the wings, and Justinian pulled away.

The furious collie stood below, barking.

✝ ✝ ✝

Justinian glided above Cameron Abbey. It glowed with torchlight, a golden brooch pinned to the velvet cloak of night.

All was quiet.

Lizard eyes, wide in the darkness, gazed down at the cruciform chapel, the octagonal chapter house, the lean-to priory, the column-clad cloister. The columns were as scrawny and irregular as Scottish thistles. Torchlight cast their thin shadows into the center of the cloister, where they converged like the spokes of a wagon wheel.

Justinian's attention shifted from the shadows to the great slab of granite beneath them. The Sacred Stone of Cameron. The cloister had been built around the rock.

Perhaps the outcropping had been the site of some great revelation. Perhaps it had been painted with the blood of a local martyr. Perhaps it would be painted again tonight.

"Seek him beneath the Sacred Stone of Cameron."

Justinian circled downward, taking a closer look. Like any granite outcropping, the Sacred Stone of Cameron hardly seemed a place one could get beneath. Still, the Dragon's orders were clear. Robert de Moffethe would be found beneath the stone.

A robed monk wandered the torchlit cloister. He chanted some tuneless devotion and, strangely, bore a club over one shoulder. A club? Surely the abbey walls and bars were proof against wolves and brigands, and aside from a Wyrm, what could descend from the skies? It betokened a grave lack of faith to…

The monk was not alone. Three others walked the cloister, one in each colonnade, clubs grasped in their fists. The clerics moved synchronously, their steps marked by a military snap.

It was an odd hour for diligence. . . . The priests chanted prayers, true, but even in Scotland, a man could speak to God without using a club. What were they guarding?

The Sacred Stone? Who would steal a twenty-thousand-ton slab of granite? More likely, they guarded what lay beneath the sacred stone.

Where would a treasurer be but in the treasury?

Justinian banked, slipping down the curtain of night until he lighted in the shadow of a great drum pillar. Tucking his wings, he flattened himself against the contours of the wall.

If the treasury lay beneath the stone, there would be a point of entry, some crevice, some false shoulder. . . . And, Scots being Scots, they'd watch that entrance hawkishly.

Justinian studied the marching monks. One gray-bearded priest gaze fixedly inward at the lower edge of the stone. His eyes didn't leave the spot as he marched along one side of the cloister. As he turned the corner, another monk strode into the colonnade to take up observation.

Ah, in that shadow lurks a passage, and beyond that passage, a treasury. Robert de Moffethe is there, or will come there.

Coiling slyly, Justinian merged with the shadows and stalked slowly across the rubble. The image of his creeping stealth beneath the watchful priests made him almost laugh. What would they call him if they saw him! Beelzebub! Lucifer! Satan!

He neared the overhang and saw a faint wedge of lantern light coming from beneath the stone. Yes, that surely was the entrance. Fetching up beside a pillar, Justinian held his breath. There would be a split second of lapsed attention when the guards rounded their corners. The dash for the opening would have to be well-timed, silent and swift.

One monk strode slowly away. The ancient chant dwindled with him. He took two more steps and vanished around the corner.

Justinian darted. Four claw-holds launched him into the faintly glowing gap. Rock scraped his belly and arms as he grappled the stone and dragged himself in. He toppled, head over heels, into a dark niche.

The Wyrm huffed as he landed. He held still, waiting for the alarm to be raised.

After moments of panting, he rose, listened,

and peered back up the crawl space. Only night showed beyond.

He glanced about him. A chiseled set of stairs descended from the landing. Wan lantern light came from below. Judging from the wet air that coursed up the stairway, this monolith ran deep.

Justinian leaned forward, sniffed the sweating stone, and began crawling down the stairs. Any man would have walked, but he was not a man, and his hind talons would have slid on the treads.

With a menacing whisper, something took flight overhead and grazed his wing tips. Justinian turned to see twin ax blades flash out from opposite pockets in the stone. They bit together above his head like a pair of teeth.

Heart hammering, the Wyrm lifted his talon from a grimy stair. The step shifted back into place. Overhead, the blades ground against each

other and withdrew. Latches furtively clicked. Springs sinuously coiled.

In the stillness that followed, reptilian nostrils sniffed the black-coated wall. A thin tongue lashed out to taste the air. The walls, ceiling, and floor here were encrusted with layer upon layer of human blood.

I shall have to be more watchful.

Watchfulness proved to be the coin of the realm. As Justinian descended into the heart of the sacred stone, he smelled more sections rank with old blood. A pair of dead-fall blocks, a portcullis, a gauntlet of poisoned darts, a trap door or two . . . With each new and deadly diversion, Justinian's estimation of the wealth below increased.

At last, the stairs let out upon a wide antechamber, done up with plaster walls, oak embrasures, gold-gilded lanterns, a musty carpet and a pair of stout doors banded and bolted in iron. The entrance to the treasury. The lock was formidable, its ironwork bands as thick as Justinian's arms.

Beyond those doors I will find the Mirror of the Loch.

Justinian withdrew to a shadowed corner and hunkered down. Robert de Moffethe would pass through these doors, whether coming or going. He would be dead moments later. Until then, the Wyrm would wait. Waiting was something he was good at. He could wait as patiently as any gargoyle on any roof.

Robert de Moffethe would come. Hours, days, months, years—he would come, and he would die.

✠ ✠ ✠

The Wyrm leapt up from his place of hiding and wrapped taloned hands and feet around the fur-stoled figure at the door. The man flung an elbow back to smash the face of his attacker, but brocade was no match for horn. The elbow came away, trailing torn cloth and red blood.

Justinian grappled the treasurer and rammed him against the blunt bolt heads of the door. Gore streamed from the man's gray-haired temple as he turned on his attacker. *Turned?*

This Robert de Moffethe is more fighter than bookkeeper.

The nobleman's face was lined with old scars

beneath an aggressive salt-and-pepper beard, and his eyes had the keen clarity of blue skies.

Time to end that clarity.

Justinian grabbed the man's throat and squeezed. Blood vessels swelled out across de Moffethe's eyes. His head seemed to enlarge with the pressure within. Justinian could kill him now and be done. The mission would be concluded, simple and quick, though he had crouched in the rock's belly for three days. Merely a squeeze of his claws, and the treasurer's head would burst apart like a pomegranate.

Still, what of the Mirror of the Lake? If the artifact was so powerful, surely Justinian should recover it and bear it back to Sterling Manor.

"Greetings, Robert de Moffethe," seethed Justinian. "I imagine you know who sent me."

The man nodded tightly, more anger than fear in his face.

"I will kill you, Treasurer de Moffethe. It is my mission. I can kill you now, or kill you after we have had time to talk."

The man hissed something between blood-limned teeth.

Justinian's grasp eased for a moment.

A small dagger leap into the Wyrm's mouth and struck his palate. The blade dug through flesh and bone and wedged there. Justinian bit down on the blade handle—and on the hand that held it. Suddenly, there was a salty spray.

Robert de Moffethe drew back his severed forearm, twin bones jutting like a pair of claws. The fight was not out of him, though. Numbly, he rammed the jetting stump into the Wyrm's gut. In shock and disgust, Justinian spit the man's hand into his face.

These Scots fight like cornered badgers.

He almost ended it then, snapping the man's neck, but that was what the treasurer wanted.

What of the Mirror of the Loch?

Claws released the man's neck and snatched his streaming arm. With bone-crunching force, Justinian squeezed the stump until the flow of blood dwindled to dribbles. De Moffethe slumped limply beside him.

Justinian growled in irritation.

With one talon stanching the blood flow, he used the other to grab the ring of keys on the man's belt and hoist him bodily to the lock.

Patient and persistent, Justinian fitted one after another of the keys into the lock.

At last, tumblers clicked. He withdrew the key and let de Moffethe slide back to the floor.

A kick sent the doors bursting inward. Darkness rolled in the cold, wet air beyond. The massive doors boomed against the inner walls. There came a good ten breaths of silence before an echo answered.

Justinian blinked and huffed. He clasped a wall lantern and wrenched it loose, then held up the light to see into the room.

It was not so much a room as a cavern—a living cave that sloped sharply away from the doors. The far walls and ceiling were lost in darkness.

Justinian smelled the distinct reek of his own kind—of ancient Wyrm flesh.

A dragon's lair?

The thought was confirmed moments later. Justinian strode down the slope, dragging the limp form of de Moffethe. His claws clinked onto gold coins. Lifting the lantern, he saw before him a mound of riches—crowns, scepters, staves, pearls, gemstones, swords, helms. Mixed among them were countless human skulls and ribs and leg bones.

"A dragon's horde," said Justinian. "The Wyrm of the Loch must once have been more than legend."

He climbed the mound of riches, awe deepening with each shifting step. Did the priesthood know this once was a dragon's lair? And why hadn't they looted it, taken the riches for the church and the glory of God?

"I'll have none of yer devil gold, neither."

Suddenly, he knew. Devil gold. The priests and locals were not thinking of dragons but of Satan. To them, this cavern of gold and bones was an entry into hell, a place meant to entice mortals to their deaths. The priests did not guard the treasure from the world, but the world from the treasure.

De Moffethe must know the truth. He must somehow have discovered the hidden history of dragons. And here, in the trove, he has found the Mirror of the Loch.

Something huge hung in the air ahead, just beyond the reach of the lantern light.

Justinian trudged atop the shifting trinkets, dragging the treasurer in his wake and holding the lantern up before him.

The wan light reached out across the cavern and brushed the far wall.

Words. They floated in the blackness. The characters were not English—even too barbaric to be Gaelic. Justinian knew them all the same. They resonated in the heart of his being like a half-remembered wish.

Ancient Dragon—the tongue of his lost people.

The characters had been painstakingly etched into the cave wall. Lines of arcane text crowded from floor to ceiling. Each letter was the height of a man, and the whole wall was the height of a dragon.

Justinian lifted high his lantern and continued toward the dim words. The letters grew from man-size to horse-size to elephant-size.

After marching across countless drifts of coin and loot, Justinian came to a great black lagoon.

On the far wall, the lines of text ran down into the murky water.

Whatever dragon laired here, thought Justinian, it used this lagoon to swim out to the loch.

He craned his neck back and, still clutching the severed arm of the treasurer, began to read the dragon's testament.

✠ ✠ ✠

It was the year 912, as the humans reckon it, when the priest John Cameron came to my loch. He was a dragon-slayer, like all his stinking brood. I am a priest-slayer, and his blood anointed my loch.

But men are like ants. When one is slain, more come to bear the body away. After John Cameron came more Children of the Crucified. They, too, bled into my waters.

They drink blood, these priests, and wash in it, so I thought it served them well to pour their blood in my loch. That's where I got the idea for the spell.

One man learned of my lair, here beneath the granite. He was another Cameron, an Iacobus. Before I could slay him, he told the others.

They have begun to dig down through solid granite. I hear their picks. I slay them in their tens, but more come. More, and more.

They will overwhelm me. It is the way of this world that vast legions of mediocrity will bear down any singular superlative. But they will not succeed until the loch is red with blood, until my spell is complete.

And so, as they dig, I carve these words. It is 1169 by the human calendar. I am the only wyrm that remains in these isles. Soon, I too will be gone, but my spell will remain. The Mirror of the Loch. Even when I die, Loch Ness shall never be truly free of dragons. . . .

✠ ✠ ✠

"So," came a gravelly voice from below, "ye have read it. Ye know what I know."

Justinian glanced down past the mangled stump, to the man who dangled beneath. Robert de Moffethe was sepulchral, his face mottled and slick with sweat. The Wyrm blinked dispassionately at his victim. "Where is it—the Mirror of the Loch?"

The man laughed. It pained him to do so. He hissed, but mustered the breath to speak. "I will not tell ye, but ye will not find it down here."

This claim was spoken so plainly that Justinian did not even think to question it. "You found it by reading these words! How can you, a mere man, read Ancient Dragon?"

Robert de Moffethe clamped his eyes. "I am a scholar of yer kind."

"A scholar or a slayer?"

"A scholar," Robert echoed, "though, anymore, scholars must be slayers. Knowledge of what ye are and what yer master seeks impels a virtuous soul to hunt ye, and slay ye."

"If you know so much about 'my kind,' who am I, and whom do I serve?"

"Ye are a blooded disciple of the Dragon—a creature of ultimate evil," said the priest blandly.

"No, not evil," Justinian replied levelly. "The Dragon is the last of an ancient, noble, and powerful line of creatures, driven into extinction by humans."

"He is that, aye," said de Moffethe. "But evil, too. Humans forced evil onto dragons, aye, but dragons came to embody it."

"Humans forced genocide on dragons," Justinian said.

Robert de Moffethe opened his wise eyes and gave his captor a look of compassion. "I canna blame ye for killing me, Wyrm. It is war. But though ye have the right to slay me, know this: yer master is evil. He desires to return to the world—and to do so he would slay any and all her creatures, including his disciples."

"You lie."

"He's already at work. He's here, a new Wyrm of the Loch—yer master. He uses the Mirror of the Loch to appear to locals and recruit them. Go see what works he does. Go see what mayhem his disciples do. Kill me, aye, but then go see for yerself if the Dragon would slay his own."

Justinian stood a moment longer, trembling with anger and uncertainty. His mind swam with this man's words.

They are only words, meant to distract me from my mission.

"Where is the Mirror of the Loch?" Justinian demanded.

"Oh, no, Wyrm. Ye'll not learn that from me. Ye'll have to find it yerself, just as I did."

Justinian released the bloody stump.

Robert de Moffethe fell to the bed of coins. Gore fountained anew from the severed arm, life sinking into the insatiable trove. In his last, shivering moments, the treasurer of the Church at Glasgow moved the streaming stump over his breast, forming the sign of the cross. And then he was gone.

Justinian stood above him a moment before spitting green bile. How could mortals be so deceived?

The first toiling twinges of transformation stole into his muscles. The mission was done, and his wyrm form was beginning to dissolve away beneath him.

No, not yet. First, the Mirror. Then I must flee.

In human form, there would be only one way out of the cave, past treacherous traps and watchful guards. In draconic form—but he couldn't stop the transformation now that it had begun.

Justinian drew a deep breath and dived into the murky pool. His wings caught the water and drove him down into the ichorous flood. He flung himself deeper, deeper.

Ah, there—a cold, strong current, bubbling ahead.

He bunched his wings near his flanks and waved them finlike. Black jets of water coursed out behind him. The current grew stronger. He nosed through its stream. One wing caught for a moment upon a lip of stone at the mouth of the waterway, but he dived deeper, pulling free.

The pressure was intense. His head creaked in its grip.

His eyes were wide open, but there was nothing to see. In the rhythm of the black tides, he could feel the smooth underbelly of stone above. His wings thrust him along, as swift as a shark.

The dead air in his lungs began to burn. The cold current deepened and strengthened. Justinian pushed into the teeth of it.

Air. He needed air. To go deeper felt wrong.

His head struck glancingly along a ponderous wall of rock. Farther down.

An ache like dull dagger points pressed into his temples.

The deepening dive was not all that felt wrong. He was changing. He could feel it.

Strength fled his legs. Hard sinews melted to butter. Hind claws fused into flat, weak feet. Fore claws smoothed and lost their jagged grip on the water. Wings shrank toward shoulders. Ribs that once could have deflected arrows became as soft as bread dough.

Still, he descended.

The air boiled in him. It had been scalding in a Wyrm's air sacs—but in the soft pink flesh of a man. To hold this air in him . . . it was molten iron . . .

In a blast of breath, he purged his lungs.

He was no longer moving. His feet and hands scooped uselessly. The water around him was suddenly warm and still. Muscles cramped and spasmed. He flailed.

Air! Air!

Blackness enveloped him.

"See, Angus!—wi'out a stitch on, sleeping like he canna even drag himself up from the lapping loch," came a young voice in the aching darkness.

The one called Angus answered. "All right, then, Michael. Ye've made up for the troubles ye stirred wi' the MacDonnell flock. Now, out of the way so I can get my eye on this drunkard."

Justinian lay very still, sensing the presence of soft-soled feet padding the gravel near his head. He breathed. Bloody foam clung to his lips. He lay still. A stick prodded his back and neck.

"Still breathing. That's good. Canna think the Dragon'd give us any powers for sacrificing what's already dead."

"The MacDonell's dead bull ought to've told ye that much."

They all laughed, a nervous group of ten or twelve boys.

One of them volunteered, "He'd be dead already but for us finding him, I'd say, so his life belongs to us, anyways."

"Hoist him high," Angus cried, "and to the Dragon's Altar. It'll be a short heave and a long dive down the waterfall!"

Hot, hard fingers grabbed Justinian's bare arms and legs. The boys struggled to haul him to their shoulders, but he violently rolled from their grip and fought free. He splashed away from them in the knee-deep water.

Staggering to his feet, he growled, "Back!"

Surprised, the lads hovered just out of arm's reach.

"Acch. He's sprayed me with something. Poison!"

It was blood from his lungs, but Justinian would take any advantage he could get. "Aye, you're poisoned, lad, and I'll breathe my poison on the rest of you if you don't stay back."

They seemed to believe it, standing in an uncertain ring just beyond the reach of the waters. It would not take them long to decide that this naked and battered man was no dragon. Of course, if he could become a dragon . . . He opened his mind to the master, but felt no surge of power, no inkling of transformation.

Angus, a head taller than the rest, stepped forward. His lean face looked toothy in the darkness. "Ye're no dragon. Ye're just an Anglish drunkard, loud and naked and thinking ye own the place. This is Scotland, and ye're a dead man."

"It'll take more than children to kill me," Justinian hissed. His thoughts lashed out for the Dragon. Nothing.

"Children?" Angus growled. "We're more than children. We've got a dragon on our side. He'll be glad to meet you. Come on, lads." He dug the heel of his boot into the gravelly shore and began sketching out a five-pointed star. A summoning circle.

Justinian laughed—just when he couldn't summon the dragon, his enemies would.

"Away with ye, MacIntoshes," came a shrill voice. "This is MacDonnell land. Ye'll not be doing yer devil deeds here."

Justinian looked toward the nearby hillside, where a torch flickered in the windy night—the shepherd lad, Ian. He was no less intrepid or foolish now than he had been three nights back.

Angus completed his star and waved one of his underlings off into the shadows. "Go home to yer mother, Ian. Ye've no business wi' this drunkard."

"As long as ye're on my land, I've all the business in the world," answered the torch-bearing youth.

"This is not your fight," Justinian shouted. "Get back. Someone is coming for you—"

Ian's torch fell to the wet grouse and guttered away into darkness. From the shadowy hilltop came his muffled protests and the sound of feet thrashing through scrub.

"I got him," cried a boy, gleefully.

Angus finished a circle around the star and waved the others into place. "Bring him. He seems to know this drunk. Might as well have two sacrifices as one."

Among the hunched young shoulders, whispered protests circulated: "Not Ian—" "—there'll be questions—" "—widow MacDonnell knows us all—"

Angus's deprecating growl won out. "What! Ye're afraid of widows! We're dealing wi' the bleeding devil, lads, and ye're afraid of widow MacDonnell?"

Two figures seized Ian and flung him into the water.

"Enough of this child's play. Summon your Dragon," Justinian challenged.

Ian turned to him and clutched his arm.

"Anglish, ye don't know what ye're saying. There is a Dragon, the Wyrm of the Loch. I've seen him myself—"

His words trailed away as the wailing chant of the ruffians began—a nonsensical rhyme the boys must have devised.

Justinian crossed arms over his chest and skeptically watched the chanting crew toe-dance around the gravel pentagram.

"Don't be frightened," he said wearily. "They have no idea what they're doing."

At first, only a choked silence answered. Then Ian whispered, "Anglish, ye couldna be more wrong."

Justinian glanced toward the shepherd boy, seeing his young, trembling form silhouetted against green-glowing water.

The Earl of Sterling blinked, thinking the light came from glow moss or a strange Scots algae. The color moved, though, in fitful currents that surged and glided and eddied and surged again. Fish?—schools of minnows? The long strings of green deepened into lavender chutes and shafts.

Justinian took a steadying step. A seething, hypnotic glow filled the water all around. It coiled, serpentine, and boiled like bile in the belly of some great monster.

They've done it, he thought. They've actually summoned the Dragon. The whole loch is a mirror in which he can appear.

Then he knew: the artifact of power was Loch Ness, itself.

The knowledge rooted him in place—the knowledge or the power of the Dragon over his minions. He stood there, as entranced as the others.

The chanting had ceased, and the toe-dancing, too.

Ian alone had kept his wits. He struggled through the turgid waters and gained the bank. Even now, if any of the others had looked, they would have seen his dim indigo outline running from the loch.

Ian no longer mattered—not to Justinian or to the bullies. Only the Dragon mattered.

He was taking shape in the loch. Enormous lizard scales tickled along Justinian's calves. Scythe-long claws slid placidly on the pebbled bottom. Ancient horns cleaved beneath the waters. . . .

The dragon rose. First, his iridescent muscles were only wind-blown waves. The billows

A nictitating membrane drew sharply down across one eye.

"Who?"

"We summoned ye, Great One," squeaked Angus. "I did. I offer ye this sacrifice." He held a shaky hand out toward the naked captive.

The Dragon blinked. Its black jowls drew back from tusklike teeth, and it seemed to smile. *"Ah, Justinian, you have run afoul of my Loch Ness youth brigade?"*

Justinian's tone held nothing but reverence. "The task is complete, my lord. The priest is slain."

"I know, Justinian. Well done." The Dragon turned its eyes back upon Angus. *"My young disciple—were you planning to sacrifice this servant of mine?"*

Angus's face was greenish. "We—we had no idea this drunkard was in yer service, Laird Dragon. No, of course we would not offer such as he."

"Then, whom?" came the resonant reply.

It was Angus's turn to blink … once… twice … "Whom?"

Before the third blink, blue-green radiance lashed out from the dragon's eyes. The twin beams sliced into Angus and shredded him. Bone, muscle, brain, and all sloughed down into so much meat. The stuff rolled slowly over, drawn into hungry waters.

"Thank you for the sacrifice, Angus," the Dragon replied. *"The rest of you, learn from his example. He was a stupid lad. I want no more stupidity from you. You are my men, now. I expect obedience. I will slay you in your beds if you disobey."*

In that moment, they ceased to be boys. Their young faces were pale and grave and hard. Whatever had once made them innocent and free had suddenly been ransomed away. They would evermore dwell in the shadow of the Dragon's wing.

As one, the young men said, "Yes, Laird Dragon."

"And now, take my loyal servant. Clothe him and feed him and give him a warm, dry bed. That is your first task. Fail in it, and one of you shall die.

"As to the second task, there is the matter of a meddlesome young shepherd, a certain Ian MacDonnell…"

rolled, gained sinew, braided their currents into rills. Here, a whisker tip emerged . . . there a back spine . . . a lashing tail . . . a tufted elbow . . . a bristling shoulder.

A horn-barbed wing lifted above the toiling waves. Its leading edge trailed a curtain of water, behind which a massive flank took shape. Slowly, majestically, the Dragon coalesced from the waters of the loch. Its wing flung back green spray, and up from the depths came a magnificent neck. Mantled in seaweed and streaming magic, the neck arched and drew after it a large mound of water. A great, hoary dragon head followed. Water drizzled from jutting horns, rolled over slitted eyes and poured from between teeth as tall as men.

"Who has summoned me?"

None among the trembling crew answered.

~finis~

86

SIR JUSTINIAN
THE EARL OF
STERLING

Born in 1394, the only son of a wealthy nobleman, Justinian was a gifted artist. He married the daughter of a nobleman and they were blessed with five healthy children. At the death of his father, Justinian came into his inheritance. He was twenty-seven.

Then came the Black Death. Wealth was no barrier to the insidious disease. Justinian, his wife and children were stricken. He was forced to watch, helpless, as his family died. Then he and his wife caught the disease. In terrible pain, terrified of death, Justinian stared into a mirror which stood in his study. It seemed to him that there was a living essence in the mirror, a Dragon that promised him eternal youth and immortality in return for his services.

He accepted the offer and swore his life to the Dragon. He then tried to force his wife to do the same, but she recognized the Dragon for what it was, and refused. Justinian watched her die in agony.

His manor gained an evil reputation, especially as time passed, his contemporaries aged, and Justinian remained young and strong. He was forced to start roaming from country to country throughout Europe in order to hide the fact that he never grew old. It was during these travels that he found out he was not alone. He met other Disciples. He also found out that he was not truly immortal. He could be killed—but only by the blade of a true knight or a sword which bears the relic of a saint in the haft of the hilt.

Down through the centuries, Justinian continued to serve the Dragon, removing those people who were threats to either the Dragon or the community of Disciples who serve the Dragon. He currently lives in the United States, where he works as a freelance artist under the name "Justinian Sterling." He is the creator of a comic book called "The Wyrm."

THE SHIFTING

When Justinian Shifts into the Wyrm, he remains approximately his same height—about six foot two inches. Leathery wings sprout from his back. Glittering scales form over his skin. His tongue is forked. His hair turns white. It juts up in front, flows down his back, rather like a dragon's mane. His eyes are red and reptilian. His fingers alter into four claws, with long, slashing nails. His legs are like the heavy-muscled back legs of a dragon. His teeth become fangs. He spits gouts of fire. He has immense strength in his legs and arms and can fly and leap great distances.

Justinian cannot control the shifting. Whenever he receives a command from the Dragon, Justinian takes the form of the Wyrm. Only by performing the assigned task can he return to his normal human appearance.

The Pimpernel Problem

by Janet Pack

"Shall we retire into the library?" Lord Antony Dewhurst's dinner had been exemplary: delicious soup, the fowl roasted juicy, English beef medium-rare to give justice to its tenderness and flavor.

Replete, Sir Andrew Ffoulkes and Sir Justin Sterling followed Lord Tony's suggestion and found seats around the well-laid hearth as their host rang for brandy. Hathaway entered and offered the men small crystal goblets. After pouring, the manservant quietly shut the oak door behind him.

"Excellent, Tony," sighed Ffoulkes. "You stock the best cellar in England."

"Percy still owns that title," Dewhurst smiled. "My collection can't compete—"

A knock interrupted. The manservant brought a card on a silver salver to his lordship.

"Zooks, speak of the devil." Lord Tony jumped up, grinning. "It's Blakeney himself." A handsome blond head poked around the door. "I'm welcome, then!"

"Of course, my good friend. Join us in a brandy!"

"Don't mind if I do." Blakeney, leader of London fashion, close friend of the Prince of Wales, rumored to be the richest man in England, strolled in and took a goblet of topaz spirits from Hathaway. Saluting the others, he draped his long body across a chair. Heavy lids made his blue eyes appear sleepy and his face look indolent.

89

Congratulations pelted him. Justin's magnificent oils had captured Dewhurst's attention little more than a year ago, after Sterling's return from Italy. Tony had introduced the artist to England's nobility, where he'd become a sensation. The invitation to join the Scarlet Pimpernel's League had come only recently.

"Sterling, did you hear about the Comtesse de Tournay and children's rescue? What a coup during this year of 1792!" Dewhurst poured himself brandy and drank, eager to launch his tale.

"I say, Tony," drawled Sir Percy. "Must we hear of that dammed Pimpernel fellow?" The nobleman's hand waved slowly as if shooing a gnat. "Those stories're swamping England. Lud, Sir Justin's heard it twenty times."

"I haven't, Sir Percy," Justin encouraged, shoving a wayward strand of naturally white hair into place. His expression, well-schooled after four centuries of practice, sharpened with interest. "Please."

Sterling's primary cause for attending tonight's dinner was to inform himself about the infamous Scarlet Pimpernel, that phantom the French termed a bandit (and other less complimentary epithets) and the English hailed as a national hero. Justin, settling back to listen, needed all the details, both as a member of the League of the Scarlet Pimpernel and to further his own plans.

Justin's assignment from his master, the Dragon of the West, had been to murder the Comtesse de Montagne, a devotee of the Dragons Beyond. The Wyrm, Sterling's murderous alter ego, had almost been trapped gloating over her body. Sharp senses had allowed the Wyrm a few second's warning, else the Scarlet Pimpernel himself might have discovered him within her locked chambers.

Since none of the League owned to knowing their leader, Sterling had no way of knowing who'd opened the door just after he'd plummeted from the window. The Wyrm had loped off down an alley. The Change returned Justin to human form moments later, pleased at remembering this murder but concerned about his near-discovery.

"A delicious story." Dewhurst rubbed hands together. "A guard named Bibot at the West Gate Barricades in Paris prided himself on spotting dis-

"That afternoon sun near boiled me. Zounds, I'm nigh done in!" He quaffed his brandy. "When I heard of your gathering, Dewhurst, I mentioned it to Marguerite. She wouldn't allow this day to quit without my bringing you invitations to our water party end of next week."

Pushing himself upright, Percy ambled from man to man, fishing in a pocket of his sapphire velvet coat and offering envelopes addressed in his wife's neat handwriting.

"Thanks, Blakeney," Justin said, his dark, mellifluous baritone trembling the crystal in hand. Some people had been known to follow his voice straight into their graves. "Saved from boredom that weekend."

One lazy eye widened slightly, one eyebrow raised. "What, not enough work to drown in? Begad!"

"No, I've just had three paintings ordered, one from the Duchess of Kent."

guises. He'd seen through makeup and rags worn by nobility and intelligentsia of France endeavoring to escape the new government. One morning, a cart, driven by a hag seen often around the knees of Madame Guillotine, drove up. Bibot questioned her, commenting on her whip, decorated with hanks of hair which, the hag claimed, belonged to dead aristos. She'd sweet-talked the trophies from the guillotine's attendant."

"Lud, disgusting!" drawled Percy, finishing his brandy and reaching for the carafe.

"When Bibot insisted on inspecting her cart, the old woman declared her grandson was in the back, sick with pox or plague. Crowd and guard gave her plenty of room to drive right through the Barricade." His ringing laugh filled the library. "The Comtesse, her son and daughter were in the cart's bottom beneath filthy rugs, so frightened they could scarce force a breath. The hag was the Scarlet Pimpernel himself!"

"Amazing!" Justin applauded. "What happened to the guard?"

The blade of Dewhurst's hand descended against the rim of his glass, a motion none of the men needed words to interpret.

"Horrible, what the French are doing to their people," murmured Sir Andrew. "I hope that never happens here."

"Can't," yawned Percy. "Odd's fish, we Brits are far too sensible nowdays to make that kind of mess." He straightened his silk cravat frothed in delicate Mechlin lace. "Sink me, the thought of another neck under Madame Guillotine makes me shudder."

"Anyone heard more about the Comtess de Montagne's death?" asked Ffoulkes.

Justin hid startlement. He named the same countess the Wyrm had killed.

"The poor clawed woman!" Tony asked, boisterous voice growing more so with excitement. "Zounds, I'd like to have sport with that animal. What a hunt!"

"The devil, surely," Ffoulkes murmured.

"Hideous subject." Sir Percy finished his brandy, stood and nodded to the company. "I have another beastly long ride ahead of me."

"I'll see you out, Blakeney," said Lord Tony.

"Don't bother. Odd's fish, I'll lay bets it's the same way I came in. And if I lose myself in this maze of castle you call a house, I'll run into Hathaway eventually and ask directions. Hopefully, before I starve. "Evening, all." He left to their chorus of good-byes.

Ffoulkes thumped down his drink. "No human would so foully treat a woman!" he spat, returning to the murder.

"Someone did, and we have no clue who," Sterling declared. "Anyone heard from our dauntless leader?"

Shrugs and shaking heads replied.

"He'll let us know," Sir Andrew said softly, hero-worship in his wide blue eyes.

"That beast will add more zest to the hunt," Dewhurst said with a smile of excitement.

"Besides the Committee for Public Safety, might we of the League have here a rival for French lives?" queried Justin.

Discussion broke out between Ffoulkes and Dewhurst. Justin dropped an occasional question or comment for appearances sake, listened the rest of the time. This was a tactic he'd used to great advantage throughout the centuries. The tightest-bound oath might slip just a little during heated debate, letting secrets escape.

Shafts of nervousness and delight twined in Justin's mind to send javelins of adrenaline through his veins. When he'd been invited to join the band of nobles in their cause to rescue a few dissident artists and upper crust from the murderous citizenry of France, he'd thought it an easy way to gain information about and access to his enemies. His sojourn in Italy had revealed that a half-dozen adherents to the Dragons Beyond resided in Paris. De Montagne was one, also the freethinker/poet Raimond de Guise, purported leader of the group. Sterling intended to kill every one. It was his duty, his honor, and his great pleasure.

This Scarlet Pimpernel would be an opponent equal to the best he'd faced in the past. Whoever the man was possessed a cool, quick mind even in close situations. His costumes were perfect, his characters fit into locale as well as finely-crafted watch parts into their case. Ffoulkes had said at dinner that the Scarlet Pimpernel could stand between two identically dressed French guards and founder them in rhetoric until they had no clear idea what they were wearing. An excellent actor despite a proclivity toward the flamboyant, he possessed an unparalleled eye for detail and a faultless ear for dialect. Most important, his intellect matched his other talents.

The man was dangerous.

But that would make killing him that much more pleasurable. Against the base of his brain the Wyrm stirred in anticipation.

Justin would have to dust his own considerable gifts. This encounter might be as entertaining as his brush with formidable Sir Francis Bacon in the late 1500s. Evading the Scarlet Pimpernel while eliminating the Dragons Beyond group could be fun. So might calculating each move against the pittance of information he received about the Scarlet Pimpernel's plans. Concurrently, he needed to keep lookout for Drokpas searching for him.

"We must all watch closely for sign of the monster," suggested Ffoulkes.

Lord Tony smiled. "Having once killed seemingly for pure joy, it may return."

"We should report to the Scarlet Pimpernel any strange circumstance or any rumor we might overhear," stated Sterling.

"And if we're confronted by this gargoyle, we must do our bravest," Andrew declared.

"It seems no ordinary animal," mused Justin. "It may take extraordinary measures to dispatch. I wonder how I might best that horror."

Jests followed. Justin Sterling was not much with weapons. His fencing showed little improvement despite the finest teachers the group could recommend—he made himself clumsy to hide his long-fostered ability. All admitted him a fine horseman. And he had lately proved himself a passable shot with a pistol.

"I hope never to see the thing," said Ffoulkes, standing. "Not even in dreams. I'll take my leave now. Excellent dinner, Dewhurst. Good night, gentlemen."

Justin, too, made his way to the door, where Hathaway fitted his dark blue cloak around his shoulders. Outside, a groom ran up with his showy dapple gray. Sterling saluted his host again, swung into the saddle and rode toward his own mansion, an hour's canter under the gibbous moon.

His "estate" was rented, if anyone could puzzle through the paperwork he'd layered to disguise reality, a modest fifteen-room two-storey stone structure, no outlying buildings and no tenants. He rented the meadows for grazing and allowed the wood to grow tangled. The fewer who knew about his comings and goings, the better. A taciturn man ran the house, a timid maid doubled as cook, and a glum groom presided over the stables. Over centuries Justin had learned to keep things simple in case a quick disappearance became necessary.

He no longer needed a Hall of Mirrors to call the Dragon of the West. A small silver-backed mirror sufficed, locked in the private study adjoining his bedroom. Tonight, he was eager to speak with the powerful beast that controlled his life. He wanted to discuss the Scarlet Pimpernel.

Justin reined in his horse on the stone drive leading to his house. The sleepy stableman reached for the bridle but the dapple tossed its head. Sterling whispered a word in the language of animals, and the horse quieted instantly. Dismounting, Sterling entered and surrendered his cape to his house man. He strode across the foyer to the stairway and the second floor, heading for his study.

Sterling slipped a small key from a ribbon beneath his shirt. He fitted it to the lock, looked both directions over his shoulders and skinned through into unrelieved darkness.

He knew exactly where candle and striker sat on a table inside the door. Lighting the taper, Justin lifted it and sat down at the desk where the mirror waited.

"I am here, Lord Dragon," he called softly.

Deep within the mirror something stirred, convulsed. A vague undulating form wreathed by smoke with coal-like eyes stared into his gunmetal gray ones. Sterling bowed, demeanor changing to that of a minion.

"I see you, my oldest and favorite servant", the dragon's oily voice, deep and unctuous, shuddered in his mind. *"What would you know of me?"*

"Great Dragon, I have chances to kill more Dragons Beyond worshippers in France," Justin said. "The rescuers I've joined will try to save them. The Wyrm will get there first."

"Good. What troubles you?"

"The group's leader, the Scarlet Pimpernel. He's resourceful, attentive, wise and quick, more a match for me than any other in...in centuries. His orders consist of what that one person needs to know. He determines who should be rescued, when, then takes himself the greatest part, successfully smuggling nobility beyond Paris under the noses of guards. After each escape, the public prosecutor finds a scrap of paper telling him who lately flew beyond reach." The artist's wide dark eyes fastened on his master. "Shall I kill him?"

"*Too valuable to us yet as an information source. Do not kill him. There will be time later if you handle things properly.*"

Justin had been certain of the opposite. "But he may ferret out who I am. He or one of his group almost saw the Wyrm."

The Dragon's sudden spite snapped in Sterling's mind like a whip. The human gasped with pain.

"*Be certain he does not. Fulfill your duty.*" His master disappeared, leaving mist in the mirror.

Sterling sat for long minutes, considering. The Paris sect must be eliminated very soon. Making up his mind to begin, he rose. Something in his waistcoat pocket rustled.

"What's this! It wasn't there before dinner." He extracted torn paper written in a disguised scrawl. The signature was a red five-lobed flower. "The Scarlet Pimpernel," he muttered. "Orders! How'd they get in my pocket?" Justin held the scrap closer to the candle.

"Charter a boat in three days for Calais," he puzzled out. "You will receive merchandise day after. Wait usual place on coast. Code word 'Dante.' Bring copy of *Comedia*, keep in pocket."

Sterling smiled. His mood soared from the darkness of his Dragon's punishment to the heights of a peregrine falcon stooping on its quarry. Despite his uncertainties, everything had placed itself. "Dante" surely meant that the poet leader of his enemies was his.

Raimond de Guise now belonged to the Wyrm.

✠ ✠ ✠

Two days later, Sterling trotted into Paris riding a sleepy-looking bay gelding hired in Calais. The barricades posed no difficulty—it wasn't people entering Paris the new government suspected.

He made his way through crowded streets to an inn he'd patronized in the past. Making himself comfortable in the coffee room, Sterling ordered pen, paper, and ink in fluent French. He wrote three notes, sealed them and hired a ragged boy recommended by the innkeeper to deliver them. Making certain the youngster understood to bring back replies, Justin watched him scamper off and settled back.

The first response came during coffee, the second after lunch, the third during the brandy Justin ordered to accompany his reading Dante's *Divine Comedy*. His gray serpentine eyes glittered. Raimond de Guise was in his house, watched by citoyen spies until orders came from Public Prosecutor Foucquier-Tinville to arrest him.

shivered daytime with passing drays and evenings from enlightened debates.

Sterling left his horse two blocks from the house, tied loosely to a public hitching post. He strolled the streets as a businessman taking his daily constitutional. Justin's eyes sketched details of buildings, cobbled avenues and people in his memory. Well-trained over the centuries, his mind sifted minutiae, searching for anything amiss.

Passing Raimond de Guise's house the first time, he spotted a person in the shadows across the street. That had to be the French government's skulker—the man was too obvious to be anything else.

There should be one other spy watching the back of the house. Justin continued his circuit of the block, then reversed himself as if he'd forgotten an appointment. Coming to the noisome lane that abutted the rear of the poet's dwelling, Sterling insinuated himself into its dusk and crept forward. Yes, one man watching the back, obviously bored at his post. Only a ragged drunk, leaning against his partner, clutched his liquid treasure tighter and glowered at the merchant with hot suspicion in his blue eyes.

Satisfied, Justin returned to the bustling avenue. Ghosting past these guards would be no challenge to a man of his experience. He would remain cautious upon gaining entrance—one more citoyen might be close to De Guise's inside door.

He smiled. After centuries of recalling only bloodmist-shrouded moments of the deaths his alter ego caused, he could finally savor near-complete memories plucked from the Wyrm's mind. The devotees of the so-called Good Dragons deserved to die. Justin's mind seethed with hatred as he recalled the teachings of his master.

Once rulers of the earth, Dragons were faced with the burgeoning onset of the Human Era. They split into two factions. Those of the Orient, cherished and worshipped almost as gods, chose to go Beyond into another dimension so their powerful presences would not taint the weaker race. Of different ideology, the Western Dragons ignored folk except when set upon by killers called knights. On rare occasions when one of their number was killed, the Dragon minority exacted vengeance.

Sterling lingered over his drink, finally tucking the book into his coat pocket. Paying for his meal, he told the proprietor to call for his horse. A stableboy brought the animal to the courtyard, and the Englishman mounted and rode into the streets of Paris.

Justin concentrated on being an integral part of the crowd. The clothing he had chosen was conservative, just elegant enough to suggest a wealthy merchant traveling to the city on business. He kept his unusual dark eyes half-lidded, unconsciously mimicking his horse's expression.

It took him more than an hour to reach de Guise's residential area. The poet lived in an older section that had become the center of Parisian intelligentsia, narrow two-storey houses having drawing-rooms whose walls

During the Dark Ages, a group of remarkably strong priests dedicated themselves to doing away with the few "brutes" left. The priests couldn't kill the most puissant of the Western Dragons, so they banished him within the Nether realm. As a few individuals including Sterling found out, the Dragon could contact some humans through mirrors. Those who agreed to serve him received immortality and were dedicated to returning their master to his rightful place as ruler of mortals and possessor of the Earth. When time came for his master's restoration, Sterling was certain his rank placed him immediately right of the great Dragon's throne.

Justin completed the circuit of the block where the alley gaped. Again he became a shadow within others. The observer at the back still kept apathetic watch; the drunks had finished their bottles and were sprawled under a bush, asleep and snoring.

De Guise's house lock posed no challenge to Sterling. He opened it with a passkey his Dragon had told him how to make. The door hinges creaked as he cat-footed into a narrow hall and peered into the tiny kitchen. No housekeeper. Justin poked his nose into the few rooms on the main floor of the house. It seemed deserted. Carefully, he made his way to the narrow enclosed stairway and started up, testing for loose treads as he ascended.

The stairs opened onto a hallway carpeted with worn Persian rugs. The Dragon's minion kept his slow, steady advance, eyes and ears alert for any sounds from below that meant he'd been seen. He also listened for sudden sounds from his prey. The house was silent except for the normal soft pops and sighs of timber as sun and shadow exchanged places on its exterior.

Sterling savored this kind of stalk before a kill, long and slow, allowing his well-honed abilities to extend themselves before the power and blood-rage of the Wyrm flooded him and the Change began. He grinned to himself. If Dewhurst could hear that!

The Western Dragon's Disciple curbed his mind. It would not do to bungle this assignment. His success rate was one reason he was the Dragon's favorite.

Sterling turned toward the door. Confronting the wooden slab, he knocked.

A thud came from within, much like a book hitting a carpeted floor. A moment of hesitation followed, then a nervous voice asked, "Qui est la!"

"Pardon," Justin replied in French. "I must ask you about the Divine Comedy."

"But you are early."

"Yes, a change in time forced us to push the schedule."

"Ah. Entrez."

Sterling touched the door handle with his fingertips. It pushed inward, he stepped inside.

The slavering hound was in mid-leap, wide molten eyes fixed on Justin.

"Zaaath!"

The command in the language of animals had immediate effect. The dog fell out of his charge and skidded on the rug, collapsing to lay with head on paws. Eyes now mirrors of confusion, they darted around the room but always returned to the visitor. A tiny whine escaped its muzzle.

"What did you do!" demanded de Guise. "Up, Caesar, get up!"

"The dog will stay until I command him to rise. Or ten minutes passes." The Wyrm twined, crowding the base of his mind. He couldn't hold off the Change. "Now, about our little comedy..." Justin smiled, eyes chill as a deep-frozen lake, and disrobed as he relinquished himself to the beast.

He could feel his muscles thicken and elongate. His face lengthened into a snout, his mouth filled with fangs. Skin became scales, eyes changed to burning coals, hands widened and grew wicked onyx claws. The fiery urge for blood motivating the wyrm replaced most of his cool mind, making him lean toward the paralyzed poet with a ringing growl that put the dog's best to shame.

"Mon Dieu!" shrieked de Guise. "I would rather face the guillotine!"

"Sink me," drawled a voice. "If it isn't the artist!"

The Wyrm whirled, snarling into the face of the blue-eyed drunk from the alley. Sir Percy Blakeney straightened into his full height, his expression behind the quirked eyebrow pale granite.

"Get de Guise!" Justin ordered the wyrm.

In one fluid motion, Western Dragon's minion turned, leaping for his victim. A strangled whine escaped the Frenchman's lips as the changed Sterling flew toward him.

"Escape plan, de Guise!" the Englishman commanded in French. "Go, man, or die!"

His words unlocked the writer's muscles, but too late. The Wyrm grabbed the lapels of the writer's jacket just as the Frenchman tried to spin toward the inside corner of the room. Claws penetrated past fabric into flesh. The beast jerked de Guise close, opening his jaws to take out the man's throat. The Wyrm's mind flowed crimson with bloodlust and drank in the sweetness of panic and impending death.

Something hit Wyrm/Sterling hard to one side of his lower back. He staggered, dropping the writer to the carpet. The wound stung at first, then in moments flamed. With a howling snarl of anguish, the Disciple whirled and tottered, regaining equilibrium with difficulty.

"Well, well, that hoary tome told truth." Percy stood with an age-dulled broadsword in both hands, blade showing fresh blood at its tip. Wyrm blood. At the crosspiece glinted an oval cabochon of clear quartz mounted over a tiny ivory-hued splinter. "Old Saint George really does hurt you."

RAGS.

Within the Wyrm, Justin turned cold. Somehow, even behind the blazing vermilion eyes and the scales, Blakeney saw and smiled. He knew, even the part about a weapon with St. George's finger bone being able to kill him.

"Oh, yes, I looked you up. You changed countries and fairly covered your tracks, but not enough for the hounds at the British College of Heraldry to lose your scent. A substantial endowment's theirs for research on Sir Justinian, Earl of Sterling, circa 1394, artist. I mustn't slight Oxford. After a prodigious search those fussy dons came up with faintly-known Tibetan dragon-worshippers called Drokpas. Good people, your sworn enemies. You won't get far in France or England even if you do escape, because I'll hunt you down."

His smile did not reach the glacial eyes. Blakeney raised the sword. "What say, old sport. Shall we lay on, claw against claw?"

The Wyrm attacked before Justinian could stop it, talons on Blakeney's right arm, muzzle driving for the redolent rags covering the Brit's belly. Percy didn't drop the sword as Sterling had hoped, although he gasped with pain. He twisted, bringing the saint-endowed weapon across his body before the Wyrm bit. The beast changed targets at the last moment to avoid metal, snapping down on tender skin beneath the armpit.

Rags ripped. Frustrated, the Wyrm spat. The flaming gout flew across Percy's shoulder, searing his dark wig on the left side, and exploded against the wall. Curtains on nearby windows flamed as sparks caught among dusty folds and ignited. The dog, until this moment pinned to the floor, barged howling out the door as ascending footsteps sounded. As another ragged man appeared, the Wyrm growled and shoved Blakeney toward the inside wall to finish him.

"Ffoulkes!" Blakeney cried, trying to pivot beyond the Wyrm's bulk. "Get de Guise out!"

Percy ducked. Somehow, the Brit turned the awkward motion to his advantage. The beast's raking claws barely drew blood from Blakeney's back, but the edge of the St. George weapon opened another lava-searing rent in the wyrm's side.

The entire outside wall and the poet's library was now aflame. Justinian could hear cries of *Au feu! Fire!* from the street. Smoke from rugs and draperies made the men cough and the Wyrm snort. Breathing already seared the lungs.

The Wyrm threw himself toward his opponent, lost in double torment of pain and the desperate need to kill. With a jaunty wave, Blakeney stepped back and slammed the door. Throwing back his head with a howl that shook the house, the beast splintered the plank, rushing into the smoke-draped hall.

His quarry had vanished. Venting another roar, the Wyrm leaped down the smoldering steps, breaking the floorboards at the bottom. Another spring from dragon-like legs sailed him into the stinking alley.

Flames threw cranky shadows in the lane. The Wyrm cast about for sign of Ffoulkes, de Guise, and Blakeney, snorting in irritation. With smoke searing his snout, he had difficulty differentiating scents. His sensitive hearing had been overwhelmed by fire and the noise of the bucket brigade out front, his excellent sight had not even a wraith to follow. Thinking he found the barest trace of familiar blood tang at the end of the lane, the beast followed it into the main street.

The beggar screamed as, from across the avenue, he saw the Wyrm emerge from the fire's glare. Needing something to kill, the Disciple pounced on the unfortunate and tore through his neck. Dropping the body, the Wyrm sprang upward.

Fresher air above the smoke revived him somewhat. The Wyrm inhaled great gasps, trying to clear nose and lungs of acrid fumes. He felt cheated. Unless his luck turned and he managed to spot Blakeney or Ffoulkes on their way through Paris, Sterling reasoned, there would be no way he could follow the trio. And likely most of the French believers in the Dragons Beyond would soon receive scraps from the Scarlet Pimpernel telling each what he or she needed to do to escape.

He knew without doubt where they'd end up but he no longer dared appear without disguise in England. At least not while Percy Blakeney lived. Justinian smiled slightly to himself, remembering the story Lord Tony had told him about the guard at the Paris barricades just a few nights before. It often took one who wears disguises well to spot another in disguise. Dewhurst had given a lesson within his narrative.

Beyond his reach now, all of them. For the second time in his life, Justinian Sterling had failed.

He could only fly for a little while without his wounds, deeply aching from the curse of St. George's touch in the steel, properly tended. They still bled and would continue to bleed in his weakened condition. Justinian himself was exhausted. He blessed his alter ego's stern constitution, but chided the beast part of himself for detouring energy into frustration.

He dreaded the outcome of his inability to kill de Guise. Sterling needed a place to lay up for a time, a place shunned by others so his cries couldn't be heard. He remembered only moments from what had happened after his last missed kill, surfacing consciousness during agony, howling and gibbering in his own urine and vomit before the delayed Change allowed him human form again. Numbing weakness in body and mind endured for a month or six weeks before he began to recover normal strength. The Dragon of the West's punishment and subsequent coldness had been cruel ice rag-ing behind snow that collected in his quaking mind. That had taken a long time to thaw.

Now he faced it again. Abandoning searching for the Scarlet Pimpernel, the Wyrm aimed for Paris's far outskirts. A mansion sitting by itself would be ideal, Justinian thought wearily. Water, a little food, and solitude—that's all he would need for the next ten days, until he emerged in human form to face punishment.

The mansion lay off the main road and had only five people in it, three drunks and a couple making love. The drunks folded about his claws as a single talon punctured their vitals. The lovers he couldn't linger over—fast had to do this time, no delicious moments inhaling many-layered odors of panic or watching fright escalate beyond capability of expression.

Shuddering now, the Wyrm carried the dead outside, beyond range of his sensitive nose. The beast/Sterling barricaded himself within the lower storey of the gutted house and waited, slicing to splinters the last of the painted wood molding previous occupants hadn't fed into the fire. He collapsed on the floor, writhing in cold sweat and burning up at the same time.

The howling began.

finis

EX LIBRIS

I, Justinian, Earl of Sterling and Brother to Dragons, have wandered our fair sphere as a Disciple of the Great Dragon of the West since the Year of Our Lord, 1421. I have done his pleasure, and taken pride in having served him well.

Since my youth, I have been blessed with an artistic gift, an ability to render my thoughts and dreams on parchment and canvas. This gift has served me well over the centuries, both as diversion and source of income....

When the Dragon first sought me out, I had no clear sight of his form and shape. He visited me in dreams and smoky mirrors. I tried to visualize him with quill and ink, but his true shape eluded my humble talent....

I have since learned that the Dragon has no true shape, Banished to the Nether World. He appears to each of his Disciples in different forms....

Even to my
eyes, over the
many centuries that
I have served him,
my perception of him has
shifted and changed. He is
the mightiest of Dragons, my
Master, the one which Man
could not kill. And someday soon, he
will return to our world and rule, and I
shall be the most favored of his servants.

Or so he has promised.

My own appearance, when the Wyrm possesses my body and I undergo the Shifting, has also changed over the centuries. But this has been a natural evolution. With each mission for my Master, with each kill, the Wyrm has become stronger, and more dominant.

It is this most inhuman appearance that I use in my artwork for the comic book I draw, "The Wyrm." As Justinian Sterling, I am renowned for the lurid stories I tell. Yet, little do my readers realize that I merely report fact, that my life is laidbefore them in four color pictures each month. It is vanity, I suppose, but I feel the need to chronicle my journeys.... And it does pay the bills.

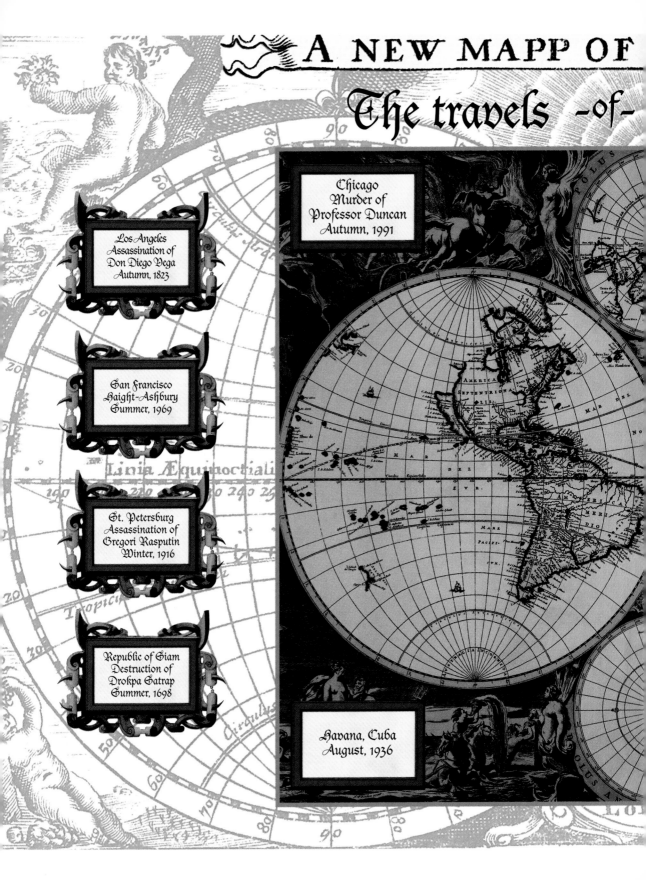

Los Angeles
Assassination of
Don Diego Vega
Autumn, 1823

San Francisco
Haight-Ashbury
Summer, 1969

St. Petersburg
Assassination of
Gregori Rasputin
Winter, 1916

Republic of Siam
Destruction of
Drokpa Satrap
Summer, 1698

Chicago
Murder of
Professor Duncan
Autumn, 1991

Havana, Cuba
August, 1936

Loch Ness
Assasination of
Robert de Moffethe
Winter, 1432

Paris, France
Encounter with
Scarlet Pimpernel
Summer, 1792

Hong Kong
Assassination of
Drokpa Priest
Autumn, 1899

Istanbul
Investigation into
Dragon Cult
Spring, 1939

Peking
Mass Execution
Shaolin Priests
Summer, 1766

The Congo River
Basin Search for
draconian Mokle-
Membe Winter, 1905

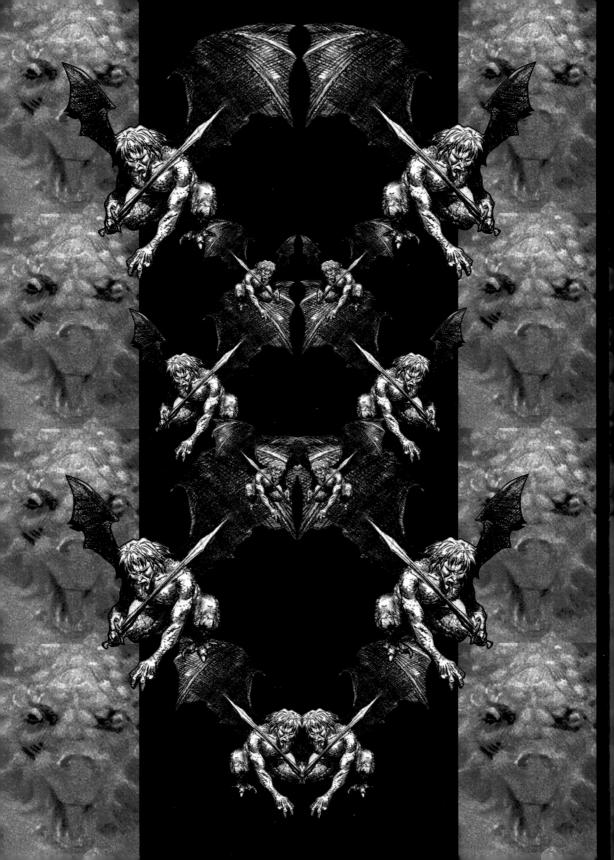